How to Hunt Buried Treasure

How to Hunt Buried Treasure

James M. Deem

Illustrated by True Kelley

Houghton Mifflin Company
Boston   1992

In memory of
my grandmother,
Ardis W. Traugh,
who taught me about
the treasures of her attic

Library of Congress Cataloging-in-Publication Data

Deem, James M.
  How to hunt buried treasure / James M. Deem ; illustrated by
True Kelley.
      p.   cm.
  Includes bibliographical references and index.
  Summary: Discusses what treasure is and how to go about finding
it.
  ISBN 0-395-58799-9
  1. Treasure-trove — Juvenile literature.   [1. Buried treasure.]
I. Kelley, True, ill.   II. Title.
G525.D36   1992   91-21749
622′ . 19 — dc20   CIP
                        AC

BP   10   9   8   7   6   5   4   3   2   1

Contents

Introduction   7

Part I. The Truth About Treasure

1. Deciphering a Fortune   12
2. Treasure Traps   28
3. Three Types of Treasure   44
4. . . . And Three More   58
5. Treasure-Tracking Techniques   72

Part II. Becoming a Treasure Tracker

6. Beginning Your Treasure Hunt   92
7. Five Clues to Consider   100
8. At the Treasure Site   120
9. Developing a Talent for Treasure   134
10. Two Lost Treasures?   156
11. On the Treasure Trail   162
    Appendix. Sample Search Agreement   181
    For Further Reading   182
    Acknowledgments and Bibliography   184
    Index   189

Introduction

Have you ever dreamed of finding a map of a deserted island, with a bold black **X** indicating the spot where a fortune lay waiting? If you dug at that precise location, you would discover a pirate's skeleton resting on a wooden chest. Inside it, a glittering treasure of gold, silver, and jewels would dazzle your eyes.

Many people have pictured this possibility. But unless you've had some experience as a treasure tracker, you may not know where or how to look. Most important of all, you may not know what treasure really is. There are many kinds besides doubloons and pieces of eight.

If you want to know how to find treasure, keep reading. The first half of the book will explain exactly what treasure is. The second half will show you how to develop your treasure-tracking skills before you start your own hunt.

But beware: This book isn't intended for anyone who wants to get rich. It's for people who like puzzles, because that's what treasure tracking is all about: solving the mystery of missing treasure. It's also about the rewards of finding portions of the past, whether they are coins or jewelry, everyday objects, or just historical information.

Anyone can be a treasure tracker; you don't need a college degree to start your hunt. But that's one problem associated with treasure hunting, as you will see: some untrained people manage to ruin the hobby for others. In this book, you will learn that some ways of tracking treasure are better than others.

There are many stories about treasure in this book. Some of the treasures supposedly are still lost, but it's possible that they were found years ago by hunters who did not report their discoveries. A few may be hoaxes.

If you find any treasure or have an interesting treasure-tracking experience, please write to me: James M. Deem, c/o Houghton Mifflin Company, Two Park Street, Boston, Massachusetts 02108.

Whatever you do, remember the search is often more rewarding than the treasure itself. Happy treasure hunting!

Part I.
The Truth About Treasure

1. Deciphering a Fortune

In January 1820, a man named Thomas Beale arrived at the Washington Hotel in Lynchburg, Virginia, and introduced himself to the hotel's proprietor, Robert Morriss. Beale struck Morriss as a well-educated gentleman who, to judge by his dark complexion, must have spent a great deal of time outdoors.

For the next two months, Beale was a popular guest at the hotel. Affable and charming, he entertained everyone with his stories, which seemed to cover every topic except one. Although Beale had registered at the hotel as being from Virginia, he never once spoke of his family. Near the end of March, he said goodbye to Morriss and checked out.

Morriss was well known for his kind nature, his loyal friendships, and his good business sense. He was generous to the poor and sympathized with their plight. According to some, no one in Lynchburg accomplished more good than Robert Morriss.

This goodness of heart had not gone unnoticed by Beale, who reappeared at the hotel in January 1822. He seemed to be the same friendly fellow as before, only this time he looked darker than ever. During his second stay at the hotel, he gave Morriss a locked iron box to safeguard.

A few months after Beale left, in March 1822, Morriss received a letter from Beale, who had just arrived in St. Louis.

In part, the letter read:

> The box left in your charge . . . contains papers vitally affecting the fortunes of myself and many others engaged in business with me, and in the event of my death its loss would be irreparable. . . . It also contains some letters addressed to yourself and . . . other papers unintelligible without the aid of a key to assist you. Such a key I have left in the hands of a friend.

By "key," Beale did not mean a key that fit a lock, but a *decoding* key, which would help a person to decipher a secret code. Beale wrote that if he or any of his friends did not return for the box by June 1832, the friend with the code-breaking key would send it to Morriss, who should open the box and read its contents.

Beale wrote that he planned to stay in St. Louis for a week or so, then head west "to hunt the buffalo and encounter the savage grizzlies. How long I may be absent I cannot now determine, certainly not less than two years, perhaps longer."

That was all Robert Morriss ever heard from Thomas Beale. Beale never returned to the hotel, and none of his friends ever claimed the box. What's more, the key was never delivered to Morriss, who eventually concluded that Beale had been killed. The box remained unopened until 1845, when Morriss decided that Beale would never return.

Inside, Morris found the following items:

1. Three sheets of paper, each covered with an assortment of numbers separated by commas. These were obviously the ciphers (that is, secret codes).

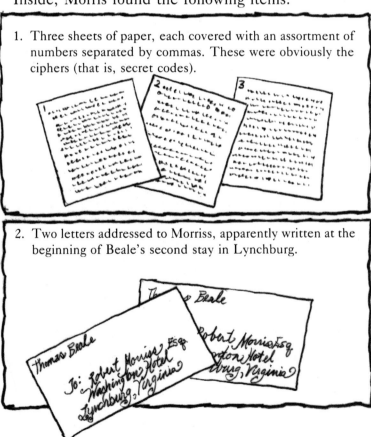

2. Two letters addressed to Morriss, apparently written at the beginning of Beale's second stay in Lynchburg.

The first letter explained how Beale and twenty-nine friends from Virginia had headed west in 1817 for a two-year hunting trip and instead discovered gold and silver in a small ravine north of Santa Fe, New Mexico, in an area that is probably now part of southern Colorado. For eighteen months, the men mined the metals, accumulating a great quantity. They decided to transport their treasure to Virginia, where they would hide it in a cave they knew from their childhood.

Unfortunately, a farmer used that cave to store vegetables, and the men were forced to select another site

in the Blue Ridge Mountains, where the treasure was eventually buried. At that point, Beale checked into the Washington Hotel for the first time, grew to trust and admire Robert Morriss, and left in March 1820 to mine more gold with his friends. Two years later, he returned with more precious metal, which he stashed in the hiding place before seeking a room at Morriss's hotel.

The treasure, Beale wrote Morriss, was to be divided into thirty-one shares, with Beale, his twenty-nine friends, and now Morriss, receiving one share each. The money was to be given to each man's next of kin. Morriss's share was "a gift, not from myself alone but from each member of our party" for his help in distributing the money.

Beale did not give a specific account of the treasure, its location, or the names of the relatives, however. That information was to be found in the ciphers in the box. Cipher #1 contained the location of the treasure, #2 described the actual treasure, and #3 listed the relatives who would inherit it.

Morriss was puzzled. Where were Beale's friends? Had all twenty-nine died without telling anyone where the treasure was buried? For that matter, where was Beale's family? Why hadn't he told them — or if he had, why hadn't they retrieved it? In fact, why hadn't the men simply shared the treasure with their families immediately? Morriss pondered these questions for a time, but he wondered more about the ciphers.

For the next eighteen years, Morriss devoted his life to deciphering the codes. Before he died, in 1863, he shared the story with someone. Exactly who this was is unknown, but we will call the person XYZ. Surprisingly, XYZ managed to solve Cipher #2. The code was difficult to crack because of its complexities, as you will see.

The first two lines of the treasure cipher read:

115, 73, 24, 818, 37, 52, 49, 17, 31, 62, 657, 22, 7, 15,

140, 47, 29, 107, 79, 84, 56, 239, 10, 26, 811, 5, 196,

308, 85, 52, 160, 136, 59, 211, 36, 9, 46,

XYZ concluded that each number represented a letter, but there were many more numbers than letters of the alphabet. Somehow, Beale had devised a code that contained more than one number per letter. What was it? Eventually, XYZ determined that the numbers corresponded to the first letter of each word in the Declaration of Independence:

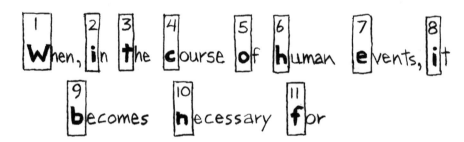

You can see that in the first line alone, the letter *i* has two codes: 2 and 8. Beale apparently numbered the Declaration of Independence up to 994, the highest number found in Cipher #2. If letters are substituted for their corresponding numbers, the first two lines of the code will look like this:

115	73	24	818	37	52	49	17	31	62	657	22	7	15
I	H	A	V	E	D	E	P	O	S	I	T	E	D

140	47	29	107	79	84	56	239	10	26	811	5	196
I	N	T	H	E	C	O	U	N	T	Y	O	F

308	85	52	160	136	59	211	36	9	46
B	E	D	F	O	R	D	A	B	O

Written out in its entirety and using appropriate spaces, the message becomes clear:

I have deposited in the County of Bedford about four miles from Bufords [Tavern] in an excavation or vault six feet below the surface of the ground the following articles belonging jointly to the parties whose names are given in number three herewith The first deposit consisted of ten hundred and fourteen pounds of gold and thirty-eight hundred and twelve pounds of silver deposited Nov eighteen nineteen The second was made Dec eighteen twenty-one and consisted of nineteen hundred and eighty-nine pounds of silver also jewels obtained in St. Louis in exchange for silver to save transportation and valued at thirteen thousand dollars The above is securely packed in iron pots with iron covers The vault is roughly lined with stones and the vessels rest on solid stone and are covered with others Paper number one describes the exact locality of the vault so that no difficulty will be had in finding it

XYZ struggled with the first and third ciphers for more than thirty years. During this time, he or she neglected family, friends, and work before ultimately going broke. In 1894, no closer to a solution to Ciphers #1 and #3 than at the start, XYZ decided to share the story of Beale and his treasure with the world, by writing an account of it. Since XYZ wanted to remain anonymous, a friend was asked to arrange for publication of the book. James Ward, the son of friends of Robert Morriss, fit the bill, and in 1894, he published an account of this story entitled *The Beale Papers*. No author's name was printed on the twenty-three-page booklet, but it was copyrighted in James Ward's name.

This pamphlet contains everything we have come to know about the three Beale codes. In fact, none of the original cipher sheets, Beale's letters of instruction, or even the iron box has survived over the years; no one knows where they are or what happened to them. The booklet has continued to interest many people, but it ends with the warning that future treasure hunters should "devote only such time as can be spared from your legitimate business to the task, and if you can spare no time, let the matter alone."

Would you like a chance to discover Beale's treasure? It's said to be worth over $20,000,000 today. Before you look at the two unsolved ciphers, take the following quiz to determine what kind of treasure tracker you are:

THE THOMAS BEALE
TREASURE-TRACKER TEST

Read each statement and decide which answer best applies:
- a. True
- b. False
- c. I don't know

1. The two remaining ciphers each contain a message.
2. Treasure trackers will not be able to locate the treasure until Cipher #1 is solved.
3. A smart treasure tracker will search the area four miles from Bufords Tavern in order to locate the treasure.
4. Some of Beale's twenty-nine friends dug up the gold and silver already.
5. Someone during the last ten years has solved the codes, recovered the treasure, and never told anyone.
6. James Ward was really XYZ.
7. Thomas Beale never really lived.
8. Thomas Beale made up the entire story and passed it along to Robert Morriss.
9. Robert Morriss made up the entire story and passed it along to XYZ.
10. James Ward made up the entire story and wrote *The Beale Papers* himself.

An astute treasure tracker would have answered each statement with "I don't know." There isn't enough proof to answer any of the statements with "true" or "false."

1. The two remaining ciphers may contain a message, but no one knows for certain.
2. Treasure trackers may be able to locate the treasure without decoding Cipher #1, but no one knows for certain.
3. A smart treasure tracker might find the treasure in that area, but no one knows for certain.
4. Any of Beale's friends could have dug up the treasure, but no one knows for certain.
5. Someone may have recovered the treasure recently, but no one knows for certain.
6. XYZ may have been James Ward, but no one knows for certain.
7. Thomas Beale may have been a fictional character, but no one knows for certain.
8. Thomas Beale may have made up the story, but no one knows for certain.
9. Robert Morriss may have made up the story, but no one knows for certain.
10. James Ward may have made up the story, but no one knows for certain.

Even though there's a great deal of confusion about
the Beale treasure, here are the two remaining ciphers:

Cipher #1: The Locality of the Vault.

71, 194, 38, 1701, 89, 76, 11, 83, 1629, 48, 94, 63, 132, 16, 111, 95, 84, 341,
975, 14, 40, 64, 27, 81, 139, 213, 63, 90, 1120, 8, 15, 3, 126, 2018, 40, 74,
758, 485, 604, 230, 436, 664, 582, 150, 251, 284, 308, 231, 124, 211, 486, 225,
401, 370, 11, 101, 305, 139, 189, 17, 33, 88, 208, 193, 145, 1, 94, 73, 416,
918, 263, 28, 500, 538, 356, 117, 136, 219, 27, 176, 130, 10, 460, 25, 485, 18,
436, 65, 84, 200, 283, 118, 320, 138, 36, 416, 280, 15, 71, 224, 961, 44, 16, 401,
39, 88, 61, 304, 12, 21, 24, 283, 134, 92, 63, 246, 486, 682, 7, 219, 184, 360, 780,
18, 64, 463, 474, 131, 160, 79, 73, 440, 95, 18, 64, 581, 34, 69, 128, 367, 460, 17,
81, 12, 103, 820, 62, 110, 97, 103, 862, 70, 60, 1317, 471, 540, 208, 121, 890,
346, 36, 150, 59, 568, 614, 13, 120, 63, 219, 812, 2160, 1780, 99, 35, 18, 21, 136,
872, 15, 28, 170, 88, 4, 30, 44, 112, 18, 147, 436, 195, 320, 37, 122, 113, 6, 140,
8, 120, 305, 42, 58, 461, 44, 106, 301, 13, 408, 680, 93, 86, 116, 530, 82, 568, 9,
102, 38, 416, 89, 71, 216, 728, 965, 818, 2, 38, 121, 195, 14, 326, 148, 234, 18,
55, 131, 234, 361, 824, 5, 81, 623, 48, 961, 19, 26, 33, 10, 1101, 365, 92, 88, 181,
275, 346, 201, 206, 86, 36, 219, 324, 829, 840, 64, 326, 19, 48, 122, 85, 216, 284,
919, 861, 326, 985, 233, 64, 68, 232, 431, 960, 50, 29, 81, 216, 321, 603, 14, 612,
81, 360, 36, 51, 62, 194, 78, 60, 200, 314, 676, 112, 4, 28, 18, 61, 136, 247, 819,
921, 1060, 464, 895, 10, 6, 66, 119, 38, 41, 49, 602, 423, 962, 302, 294, 875, 78,
14, 23, 111, 109, 62, 31, 501, 823, 216, 280, 34, 24, 150, 1000, 162, 286, 19, 21,
17, 340, 19, 242, 31, 86, 234, 140, 607, 115, 33, 191, 67, 104, 86, 52, 88, 16, 80,
121, 67, 95, 122, 216, 548, 96, 11, 201, 77, 364, 218, 65, 667, 890, 236, 154, 211,
10, 98, 34, 119, 56, 216, 119, 71, 218, 1164, 1496, 1817, 51, 39, 210, 36, 3, 19,
540, 232, 22, 141, 617, 84, 290, 80, 46, 207, 411, 150, 29, 38, 46, 172, 85, 194,
39, 261, 543, 897, 624, 18, 212, 416, 127, 931, 19, 4, 63, 96, 12, 101, 418, 16, 140,
230, 460, 538, 19, 27, 88, 612, 1431, 90, 716, 275, 74, 83, 11, 426, 89, 72, 84,
1300, 1706, 814, 221, 132, 40, 102, 34, 868, 975, 1101, 84, 16, 79, 23, 16, 81, 122,
324, 403, 912, 227, 936, 447, 55, 86, 34, 43, 212, 107, 96, 314, 264, 1065, 323,
428, 601, 203, 124, 95, 216, 814, 2906, 654, 820, 2, 301, 112, 176, 213, 71, 87, 96,
202, 35, 10, 2, 41, 17, 84, 221, 736, 820, 214, 11, 60, 760.

Cipher #3: Names and Residences.

317, 8, 92, 73, 112, 89, 67, 318, 28, 96, 107, 41, 631, 78, 146, 397, 118, 98, 114, 246, 348, 116, 74, 88, 12, 65, 32, 14, 81, 19, 76, 121, 216, 85, 33, 66, 15, 108, 68, 77, 43, 24, 122, 96, 117, 36, 211, 301, 15, 44, 11, 46, 89, 18, 136, 68, 317, 28, 90, 82, 304, 71, 43, 221, 198, 176, 310, 319, 81, 99, 264, 380, 56, 37, 319, 2, 44, 53, 28, 44, 75, 98, 102, 37, 85, 107, 117, 64, 88, 136, 48, 154, 99, 175, 89, 315, 326, 78, 96, 214, 218, 311, 43, 89, 51, 90, 75, 128, 96, 33, 28, 103, 84, 63, 26, 41, 246, 84, 270, 98, 116, 32, 59, 74, 66, 69, 240, 15, 8, 121, 20, 77, 89, 31, 11, 106, 81, 191, 224, 328, 18, 75, 52, 82, 117, 201, 39, 23, 217, 27, 21, 84, 35, 54, 109, 128, 49, 77, 88, 1, 81, 217, 64, 55, 83, 116, 251, 269, 311, 96, 54, 32, 120, 18, 132, 102, 219, 211, 84, 150, 219, 275, 312, 64, 10, 106, 87, 75, 47, 21, 29, 37, 81, 44, 18, 126, 115, 132, 160, 181, 203, 76, 81, 299, 314, 337, 351, 96, 11, 28, 97, 318, 238, 106, 24, 93, 3, 19, 17, 26, 60, 73, 88, 14, 126, 138, 234, 286, 297, 321, 365, 264, 19, 22, 84, 56, 107, 98, 123, 111, 214, 136, 7, 33, 45, 40, 13, 28, 46, 42, 107, 196, 227, 344, 198, 203, 247, 116, 19, 8, 212, 230, 31, 6, 328, 65, 48, 52, 59, 41, 122, 33, 117, 11, 18, 25, 71, 36, 45, 83, 76, 89, 92, 31, 65, 70, 83, 96, 27, 33, 44, 50, 61, 24, 112, 136, 149, 176, 180, 194, 143, 171, 205, 296, 87, 12, 44, 51, 89, 98, 34, 41, 208, 173, 66, 9, 35, 16, 95, 8, 113, 175, 90, 56, 203, 19, 177, 183, 206, 157, 200, 218, 260, 291, 305, 618, 951, 320, 18, 124, 78, 65, 19, 32, 124, 48, 53, 57, 84, 96, 207, 244, 66, 82, 119, 71, 11, 86, 77, 213, 54, 82, 316, 245, 303, 86, 97, 106, 212, 18, 37, 15, 81, 89, 16, 7, 81, 39, 96, 14, 43, 216, 118, 29, 55, 109, 136, 172, 213, 64, 8, 227, 304, 611, 221, 364, 819, 375, 128, 296, 1, 18, 53, 76, 10, 15, 23, 19, 71, 84, 120, 134, 66, 73, 89, 96, 230, 48, 77, 26, 101, 127, 936, 218, 439, 178, 171, 61, 226, 313, 215, 102, 18, 167, 262, 114, 218, 66, 59, 48, 27, 19, 13, 82, 48, 162, 119, 34, 127, 139, 34, 128, 129, 74, 63, 120, 11, 54, 61, 73, 92, 180, 66, 75, 101, 124, 265, 89, 96, 126, 274, 896, 917, 434, 461, 235, 890, 312, 413, 328, 381, 96, 105, 217, 66, 118, 22, 77, 64, 42, 12, 7, 55, 24, 83, 67, 97, 109, 121, 135, 181, 203, 219, 228, 256, 21, 34, 77, 319, 374, 382, 675, 684, 717, 864, 203, 4, 18, 92, 16, 63, 82, 22, 46, 55, 69, 74, 112, 134, 186, 175, 119, 213, 416, 312, 343, 264, 119, 186, 218, 343, 417, 845, 951, 124, 209, 49, 617, 856, 924, 936, 72, 19, 28, 11, 35, 42, 40, 66, 85, 94, 112, 65, 82, 115, 119, 236, 244, 186, 172, 112, 85, 6, 56, 38, 44, 85, 72, 32, 47, 63, 96, 124, 217, 314, 319, 221, 644, 817, 821, 934, 922, 416, 975, 10, 22, 18, 46, 137, 181, 101, 39, 86, 103, 116, 138, 164, 212, 218, 296, 815, 380, 412, 460, 495, 675, 820, 952.

Are you still interested in solving the Beale cipher? Here are some tips:

1. Be sure to work on Cipher #1 first. It's more important to find out where the treasure is than who the relatives are. Be warned, however; many people believe that Cipher #1 doesn't contain an exact location.

2. Assume that Cipher #1 will be solved in the same way as Cipher #2, which means that a piece of writing will provide the key. Therefore, you must locate a document with which Beale would have been familiar. Use the original form of the document, rather than the modern version, since spelling and wording may have changed. Number each word in the document up to number 2906 (the highest number used in Cipher #1). Then substitute the letters that correspond to the numbers in the cipher.

3. Make sure you can devote a lot of time and energy to the solution. Remember that no one has admitted to deciphering either code — and many people in recent years have used computers for assistance.

4. If you are serious about locating Beale's treasure, you should probably read Peter Viemeister's *The Beale Treasure: A History of a Mystery* for more information. You may also want to join the Beale Cypher Association (P.O. Box 975, Beaver Falls, Pennsylvania 15010). Members of this organization are dedicated to decoding the ciphers; they also share the results of their work with other members.

5. Finally, before you devote yourself to the recovery of this treasure, are you sure it really exists? Many researchers aren't even convinced that Beale was a real person. Others believe that he lived but lied about the treasure, as a kind of practical joke. Still others are certain that he was a friend of the pirate Jean Lafitte and buried Lafitte's treasure rather than his own.

What is the truth? No one knows. That's why, before you go hunting, you need to know the facts about treasure.

2. Treasure Traps

Finding your fortune won't be easy, especially if you don't know the truth about treasure. Here are five traps people fall into when they think about finding treasure.

Treasure Trap 1: Most treasure was buried by pirates

Many people associate pirates with treasure. They think that thousands of pirates sailed the seas and buried every fortune they stole under a palm tree on a desolate beach. These same people have a mental picture of mostly European pirates, who lived between 1500 and 1800, even though the world's oceans have known piracy since the time that shipping began.

The truth is that European pirates rarely buried any treasure at all. Yes, pirates were in the business of plundering rich cargoes from other ships. They were often hired by their own governments to attack ships from other countries. For example, English pirates were hired to find and rob French ships. But what many people don't know is that pirates lived by a code of honor.

Pirate captains relied on many men to sail the ship. Their only pay was a share of any booty they recovered. Harvard professor Robert C. Ritchie, who spent a great deal of time studying pirates, discovered that men who became pirates

did so because they wanted money. As soon as possible after capturing a prize they insisted on dividing the loot, which they could then gamble or carry home. The idea of burying booty on a tropical island would have struck them as insane, especially since all the men on board would demand to know the "secret," which would then be no secret.

But what about all the stories of pirate treasure? Robert Louis Stevenson's novel *Treasure Island* probably planted this idea first. Over the years, many movies, cartoons, and comic books have been based on that popular book, further spreading the myth of buried treasure. Also, many captured pirates, facing a death sentence, suddenly confessed to burying huge amounts of gold that could be located only if the pirate were allowed to live. Courts seldom believed such accounts.

For example, shortly before he was executed on Friday, May 23, 1701, Captain William Kidd confessed that he had buried a treasure of £100,000 somewhere in the West Indies. Authorities, however, had no reason to believe that he had buried any treasure, so they carried out his hanging. This hasn't stopped many people from buying "treasure maps'" that show the location of Captain Kidd's loot. To this date, no one has found any treasure associated with Kidd or his men, though many have claimed otherwise.

In 1872, a Mr. Garretson and another man were digging a ditch on the farm of Dick Thompson in Cold Spring, New Jersey, when they discovered a chest supposedly bearing the name of Captain Kidd and containing worn coins dated 1604. Unfortunately, their discovery turned out to be a complete hoax, but not before many people had started digging more ditches for Thompson.

One pirate whose treasure *was* discovered, according

31

to writer Edward Rowe Snow, was Jean Lafitte, who ran a smuggling operation along the Gulf Coast in the early 1800s. At one point Lafitte supposedly married a young woman. She died soon after their marriage and the grieving Lafitte was said to have buried a chest of her keepsakes and a thousand pieces of eight near her grave. One of his lieutenants, Joni Benuit, drew a map of the secret location, but none of the pirates ever returned to claim it, perhaps because the treasure honored Lafitte's dead bride.

In 1910, however, Dr. Joe Wooten found a treasure map hidden in a cave along the Rio Grande. How Wooten was tipped off to search this cave was never revealed, but he was convinced that the map had been made by Benuit. It was scratched on slate, its surface covered with indecipherable marks until viewed from a sharp angle. Only then did the map and some writing become visible, indicating that Lafitte's treasure would be found on an island.

For the next two summers, Wooten sailed the Gulf Coast between Louisiana and the Yucatan searching for an island that matched the one sketched on the slate. He was almost ready to give up when he discovered that Benuit had drawn the island in reverse, so that the slate map had to be reflected in a mirror to be read properly. Once he realized this, Wooten was able to identify Matagorda Island, off the coast of Texas.

Along with two friends, Wooten explored the supposed treasure site: it was desolate and larger than he had expected. Day after day, the men searched the area, finding nothing, until Wooten noticed a log that had been sawed in half. Someone had been on this island before. *Could it have been Lafitte and his men?* Wooten wondered.

They began to dig and quickly uncovered more cut timber. On August 21, 1914, they discovered a heavy chest. In all, it took four days to recover the treasure, mostly by chiseling a hole through the thick wood. Wooten was eventually able to pick the lock and open the chest's lid. Besides gold coins dated 1797, the chest contained a music box, several toys, and garments, including Madame Lafitte's wedding dress. Because the chest was heavy, Dr. Wooten and his friends reburied it after packing the gold in three smaller chests. Back home, each man cashed in his share for about $50,000.

When Edward Snow heard about Wooten's discovery some thirty-two years later, he went to Matagorda Island in search of Lafitte's chest. He found that a local resident had retrieved it and was storing driftwood in it.

Snow purchased the chest to add to his collection of pirate memorabilia and soon discovered that it contained a secret compartment — and twenty-six additional gold coins, which more than covered his purchase price.

Of course, not everyone believes this tale. Some researchers who have studied Lafitte's life are convinced that he never married, let alone buried a chest on Matagorda Island.

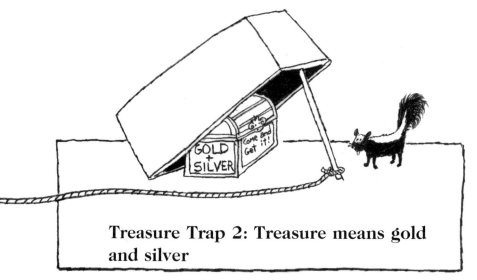

Treasure Trap 2: Treasure means gold and silver

Related to the first treasure trap is the idea that real treasure must be glittering gold or silver, or it can't be valuable. In fact, most gold and silver items that are unearthed are far from sparkling. They're covered with dirt and grime and need to be carefully cleaned.

One man who fell into this trap at first was Kip Wagner. Soon after he moved to Wabasso, Florida, Wagner began to hear stories about old coins that regularly washed up on a nearby beach. He decided to have a look for himself during his spare time.

Since he knew nothing about treasure hunting, he thought he would find shiny coins scattered on the sand. One day, though, a local resident showed him a few coins he had found: they were black and irregularly shaped and looked like pieces of scrap metal. Now that he knew what to look for, Wagner began combing the beach regularly. Eventually* he discovered more than forty coins — mostly pieces of eight, an old Spanish silver coin, and none dated later than 1715. In time, this led to the detection of a long-lost Spanish shipwreck.

Treasure, you will discover, is defined by the person searching for it. One person's treasure might be a gold coin. Another's may be an old toy car similar to those produced by Hot Wheels or Matchbox today. Millions have been made and sold since the early 1900s. Originally made of tin plate, they were later die-cast in metal. Many of the tin-plate cars cost only a penny, and their life span was quite short. Today, however, a car like this can sell for almost $100. Even so, someone cleaning a dusty attic might consider that scratched and worn toy a piece of junk and throw it away.

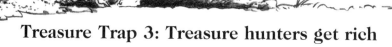

Treasure Trap 3: Treasure hunters get rich

Nothing could be further from the truth. In fact, most treasure hunters are satisfied to find anything regardless of its value. Many won't even sell their discoveries. They simply add them to their personal collections of found treasure.

The largest and most valuable treasures seem to be found in sunken ships. But people who manage to locate a sunken treasure — either through research or good fortune — usually have to spend a considerable sum of money to bring it to the surface. Sometimes the amount needed to recover a shipwrecked treasure is well over $1,000,000! Only a very rich person or a large group of people who share all the expenses (and then divide the treasure) can afford such an undertaking. For example, former chicken farmer and treasure tracker Mel Fisher spent $10,000,000 — not to mention sixteen years of research — to find the *Nuestra Señora de Atocha,* a Spanish ship that sank off the coast of Florida in 1622. The expenditure of money and time paid off on July 20, 1985, when the *Atocha* was discovered. The ship's treasure — silver bars, gold coins and chains, gold and silver tableware — proved to be worth almost $375,000,000. However, the search also cost Fisher's son and daughter-in-law their lives, when they died in a boating accident during the recovery operation.

36

Even if a treasure tracker has the good fortune of finding something valuable, he or she must pay tax on any item sold. That tax can be costly and sharply diminish the fun of treasure hunting. It also explains why treasure hunters often start collections and rarely sell what they find.

One treasure that cost a man everything in his search for it was the Buzzard's treasure. In the early 1700s, Oliver Le Vasseur, nicknamed the Buzzard, was hired as a pirate by King Louis XV of France. Although he was to attack ships belonging to France's enemies, the Buzzard soon began robbing French ships as well, and a reward was offered for his capture. For ten years, he managed to escape, but in 1730 he was caught and sentenced to be hanged. As he climbed the scaffold, he threw a parchment scroll to the crowd awaiting his execution. The paper contained twelve lines of code, including some numbers and a small diagram, which supposedly indicated an island where the Buzzard's treasure could be found.

Somehow, a copy of the parchment survived and in 1920 came into the possession of Mrs. Charles Savy, who lived on Mahé, one of the Seychelles Islands, in the Indian Ocean. Mrs. Savy knew that the Buzzard and other pirates had used Mahé as a source of food and water. She also found two buried coffins, containing bones and gold earrings like those worn by pirates. She thought that the Buzzard's treasure would be found on

Mahé, but she could not decipher the code.

In 1949 she met Reginald Cruise-Wilkins, who had come to Mahé to recuperate from an illness. When she told him about the Buzzard's treasure, he was so fascinated that he attempted to solve the puzzle of the parchment. In all, he worked on the cipher for twenty-eight years and managed to solve eleven of the twelve lines. He uncovered a beautiful stone statue of a woman, and a cave in which someone had carved the outlines of a coffin and a mummy. At one point, he had forty-eight employees engaged in searching for the treasure. They set explosives and drilled holes wherever he commanded. But, without unraveling the meaning of the last line, Cruise-Wilkins could not uncover the treasure. In 1977, he died penniless, without disclosing anything about the treasure.

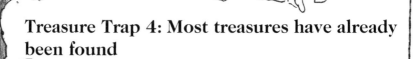

Treasure Trap 4: Most treasures have already been found

Many treasures remain to be found; in fact, there's likely to be one near you. According to writer Howard M.

Duffy, you have a good chance of finding a small treasure — one that is known by just a few local residents, who have never had the opportunity or inclination to track it down. This treasure will not make you a millionaire; it may not be worth much money at all. But some type of treasure is waiting, if you have the time and energy to look.

Residents of Carter County, Kentucky, might be on the lookout for an old silver mine, according to writer Michael Paul Henson. It is said that in 1745 a young Cherokee named Huraken found a vein of silver near Smokey Creek. Since he was in love with Manuita, the daughter of the tribe's chief, he kept his discovery secret so that he could make silver ornaments for her.

Some time later, Huraken went on a hunting party. After the men failed to return, the chief assumed that they had died and prepared to move his people farther south. Distraught at the thought of leaving Huraken behind, Manuita jumped off a cliff towering above Cave Branch Creek and died.

Manuita had made a tragic decision, for Huraken was still alive. He had been busy mining enough silver to make a tomahawk, a present to persuade Manuita's father to permit their marriage. As Huraken hurried to deliver the silver present, he discovered Manuita's body. Instead of telling the chief, he buried her in X Cave, which now is located in the Carter Cave State Resort Park.

When the chief was told about the death and burial of his daughter, he accused Huraken of killing her and sentenced him to death. As his last wish, Huraken asked to see Manuita's grave again. He was taken to X Cave and allowed to enter alone. When he didn't return, the Cherokees sealed the entrance.

Is the story of the silver mine fact or fiction? Henson believes that the story has been confirmed, based on a number of events. First, in 1783 the remains of a Cherokee woman were found buried in X Cave; her grave can now be seen on a tour of the Carter Caves. Second, a local resident discovered a silver tomahawk at the foot of a cliff near Smokey Creek. Third, a number of men in the area counterfeited silver dollars from 1812 to 1816, supposedly using silver from the mine. Finally, two other individuals have found bars of silver in the area.

As for Huraken, no one knows what happened to him. But his silver mine, according to Henson, "is believed located on Smokey Creek. By obtaining permission from the landowner, searches for the mine can be conducted." Remember that it is just one of thousands of treasures waiting to be discovered.

Treasure Trap 5: Only fools — or greedy people — look for treasure

As you've already read, most treasure trackers don't set out to become millionaires. This doesn't mean, however, that they are foolish for looking. In fact, trackers are usually smart people who search for much more than wealth. Some look for historical information. Others may even return what they find to the original owner. Still others are called upon by neighbors, or even the police, to locate lost objects.

One colorful tracker by the name of Hardrock Rick Farmer performed such a service for Laddie Martin of Salt Lake City, Utah. Farmer, who owns a treasure-hunting supply store, was approached one day by Martin, who inquired about purchasing a metal detector.

"What are you going to be looking for?" Farmer asked.

"Buried silver," Martin replied.

Twenty years ago, Martin bought some silver coins

and bars from a salesman, who suggested that he bury them until he was ready to retire. He took the salesman's advice and buried the silver in his backyard. Now that he was ready to retire, he was desperate to find the silver — only he couldn't locate it. He had dug up parts of his backyard and found nothing.

Farmer agreed to help. First, he took a look at the yard: it held a small workshop, two cement pads on which a boat and a trailer were parked, and a grassy rectangle. Then he turned on his metal detector and went into action. He searched the area but found nothing except a few nails and bottle caps.

As it turned out, Martin's memory was wrong. He had buried the silver at night, years before he had poured the concrete for his boat pad. Farmer eventually found the cache of silver — buried almost four feet beneath

42

the concrete. Using his trusty metal detector, Farmer scanned the boat pad. Suddenly, he heard a strange signal through the detector's headphones; it was "a mixture of good, strong, deep silver signals, then double beeps and squeaks." The men removed a chunk of the concrete and located the silver: it was in perfect condition, still wrapped in plastic bags and worth almost $3000.

Metal Detector

3. Three Types of Treasure

LOST, HIDDEN, AND CRIMINAL TREASURE

Now that you know the truth about treasure, you may want to find some. But finding treasure doesn't necessarily mean that it's yours. The old saw "Finders Keepers, Losers Weepers" is not always true when it comes to treasure. What you can and can't keep is determined by the type of treasure, the reason it was hidden, and the location of your search.

The law is quite complicated and varies from state to state, but following the Three Golden Rules of Treasure Tracking will help.

45

THE GOLDEN RULES
OF TREASURE TRACKING

1. *Make sure you aren't trespassing.* Not only should you get permission from a landowner to conduct a search, you should put your agreement in writing. A sample agreement form can be found in the Appendix.

2. *Try to return the item.* If the treasure can be traced to an owner who did not intend to discard it, be honest and return it. You may get a reward. If you find something valuable that does not have an identifiable owner, proceed to the third rule.

3. *Don't broadcast your discovery.* If many people hear about your good fortune, they may claim that what you found was theirs. That may make you wish you had never gone treasure tracking.

Now that you know the rules, you're ready to read about six types of treasure waiting to be found.

Treasure Type 1: Lost treasure

The most common type of treasure is an object that someone has lost. This loss can be accidental (such as a child dropping a coin as he or she runs across the field) or tragic (a gold-laden ship sinking in a hurricane). Everyday treasures can be misplaced or forgotten. Many people are interested in finding lost coins or jewelry, because they are worth some money. Or perhaps the discovery simply kindles their imagination.

Treasure tracker James Brewer and his friend Doug Patterson were searching the site of the Civil War battlefield Averasboro, in eastern North Carolina. They planned to concentrate their hunt on the grounds of an old plantation house that served as a hospital for wounded soldiers.

In a letter written about a month after the battle, sixteen-year-old Janie Smith, whose family owned the plantation, described the March 1865 event vividly:

> Ambulance after ambulance drove up with our wounded. One half of the house was prepared for soldiers . . . , but every barn and out house was filled and under every shed and tree tables were carried for amputating the limbs. . . . The blood lay in puddles, the groans of the dying and the complaints of those undergoing amputation was horrible. The painful impression has seared my very heart. I can never forget it.

One hundred twenty years later, Brewer and Patterson found many artifacts related to the battle. They also found something else: a clear glass locket, mounted on brass. Inside the glass dome was a clock face, the hands painted to show 1:22.

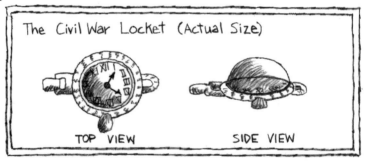

The men believed that the locket must have been dropped by one of the soldiers during the battle, but they wanted proof. For more than a year, they researched the origin of the locket, but no one had ever seen one like it—until Brewer met Floyd Pope of Nottoway Courthouse, Virginia. Pope not only recognized the locket, but had found one exactly like it, except that a different time was painted on the clock face. However, he had not determined its purpose.

Brewer was so interested in uncovering more information about the locket that he wrote an article about his find for a treasure magazine. He asked the magazine's readers to help him answer a few basic questions: Did Civil War soldiers wear the lockets? If so, what did the time on the clock face signify?

As Brewer concluded:

> I can just picture a mortally wounded soldier, lying next to that oak tree in front of the Smith house. It's the afternoon of March 16, 1865, and in his last agonizing moments, the young soldier clutches [the locket]. He breathes his last, thinking of family and home, then his hand falls to his side and the locket drops into the grass. There it lies . . . until that summer morning when Doug heard a familiar "beep" and recovered the lost locket.
>
> I can't prove that's what actually happened, but I sure would like to know.

LAWS on LOST TREASURE

The finder of a lost item is legally obliged to return it to the owner. If the owner is unknown, however, the finder may keep it. For example, if a girl could prove that the Averasboro locket belonged to her great-great-grandfather, Brewer and Patterson would have to turn it over to her or face a potential lawsuit. It's unlikely, though, that anyone could substantiate such a claim.

Treasure Type 2: Hidden treasure

Treasure can be hidden for many reasons. Sometimes people mistrusted banks and wanted access to their money immediately; they often hid it in their houses or buried it in their yards to keep it ready and available. Other times people did not want a record of the fortune they had amassed. Children often hid their own treasures, such as glass jars filled with small coins, only to forget to recover them. Such hidden treasures are called *caches*.

One cache was reportedly hidden by a tall, stocky hermit who lived on Isle au Haut, an island off the coast of Maine. One day in the summer of 1865, Henry Haggman was exploring the sparsely populated island when he became lost. Luckily for Haggman, he was discovered by the hermit, who escorted him to a remote log cabin. He told Haggman that he did not want the location of his cabin to be revealed. When Haggman promised to keep the secret, the giant man surprised him with another statement.

"I am sixty-nine years old now," he said, "and I

would say that probably I will not live more than fifteen more years. Perhaps, if you could come back about 1880, I might not mind what you reveal to the world."

This strange request stayed in Haggman's memory. In 1879, he returned to the island and with some difficulty located the cabin. This time its door was locked and its windows were boarded up. Haggman broke into the cabin through a window. There was no sign of the hermit, but one table held a box, with a message written on the lid: "To be opened by Henry Haggman only."

Inside the box, Haggman found a small package and another note. It read:

It is my hope you will return some day to this cabin and find this message. It is now 1876, many years since your visit. My last days are now approaching. I am sealing up this cabin. With your ingenuity I trust you will find a way to break in, for I know how curious you were. . . .

One thing, however, you must carry out. I warn you not to stay in the cabin or on the island more than forty-eight hours. Unless I have miscalculated, this cabin should be entirely destroyed within a few days of your leaving it.

You will not be blamed for what will take place. All you will have to do is to throw open the long trap door in the roof. Do not open anything else in this box until you arrive at your home.

Haggman opened the trap door and returned to his home in Boston before examining the package. It contained a letter that related the tragic events of the hermit's life. Once he had been a successful stockbroker in

Boston. Then his wife left him for another man. Heart-broken, he withdrew $50,000 in gold from his bank, placed it in an iron chest, and left Boston. He found an abandoned house and barn in Bolton, Massachusetts, where he decided to hide his fortune in a well. He attached the chest to a long chain and fixed the chain to an eyebolt drilled into one of the stones that lined the well. A few days later, he went to live on Isle au Haut in total solitude.

The hermit's letter gave Haggman permission to retrieve the gold. It also explained why he wanted the cabin's trap door left open: a carefully positioned powerful lens attached to a nearby tree would, when the trap door was open, direct a strong beam of sunlight onto a pile of dried leaves in the cabin and set it on fire. The hermit wanted to destroy all traces of himself, although why he wanted Haggman to inherit the gold is never clarified in any of the accounts of the treasure. Sure enough, Haggman read that a forest fire had been spotted on Isle au Haut a few days after he had opened the trap door.

Haggman was able to locate the old farm near Bolton without any trouble. He also found the well and the chain. But when he tried to pull the chain, and the heavy chest attached to it, he discovered that it was mired in

52

layers of mud at the bottom of the well. After quite a struggle, he managed to free the chest and raise it a few feet above water level.

Twenty more feet, he told himself, *and the gold will be mine.* He gripped the chain tightly and pulled again. But the chest snagged against a stone in the wall, and the chain slipped from his grasp, cutting his hands.

According to the story, Haggman gave up, since he valued his health more than the gold. Neither he nor his surviving relatives tried to recover the gold. The story raises some interesting questions. Why didn't Haggman get help from friends or relatives? Why didn't he hire someone to try again? Is the gold still there?

In 1963, Interstate 495 was constructed in the vicinity of Bolton; this required demolition of the abandoned house and barn. If the well exists, it is located near the intersection of State Highway 117 and Interstate 495. It may be so close, some say, that it now lies underneath the interstate.

LAWS on CONCEALED TREASURE

If a cache of gold coins is purposefully hidden by its owner and is discovered by someone else, the coins legally belong to the original owner or his or her heirs. In Haggman's case, if he had found the coins, the hermit's next of kin might have claimed the gold as rightfully theirs. Even today, should someone find the coins in the well, the hermit's heirs have a legal right to them, unless Haggman's heirs could prove that the hermit intended Haggman to have the coins.

Treasure Type 3: Criminal treasure

Criminals of all kinds have stolen money and, fearing capture, buried it to speed their escape. They intended to come back to recover it later, when the coast was clear. Sometimes their plans were thwarted by a long prison term and a failing memory. Others were killed before they could return. As a consequence, many criminal treasures have yet to be found.

One reported treasure was buried in 1862 by a gang of bandits who stole more than $100,000 in army payroll money. As with most treasure tales, this story has many versions, including the one that follows.

These robbers were already notorious for crimes they had committed in Sacramento, California, in 1847. By 1862, though, they had moved to eastern Colorado and were living quiet lives as farmers, sheepherders, or cattle ranchers. Still, they decided to join together for one last robbery: a poorly guarded U.S. Army payroll headed for Denver. They planned their final robbery carefully, intending to divide the money and head east, most likely to Chicago.

Their plans were ruined, however, when they found that the stagecoach was accompanied by four armed guards. They grabbed the payroll, but only two of the gang survived the shoot-out and they were quickly pursued by a posse. Rather than travel with such a heavy quantity of gold coins, the two robbers decided to bury them. A few miles east of Clifford, Colorado, they dug three shallow trenches in a circular formation. They filled the trenches and packed the earth on top to make it look as if three people had been buried in shallow graves. A rock resembling a tombstone was placed on each mound. On two of the stones, they chiseled their names and the date "1847." They carved the word "unknown" on the third stone. Exactly why they went to

the trouble of preparing three graves is unknown, but perhaps they hoped that the posse would think they had been killed in a gunfight. Finally, at the center of the circle, they dug a large hole in which they buried their

"Dutch oven" A large heavy pot

loot in three Dutch ovens. Then they departed.

No one would ever have known about the treasure if a stranger from Chicago had not come to Clifford in 1884 and found a place to stay with sheep rancher James Will. The man spent most of his time walking through the barren prairie east of town. When he could not find whatever he was looking for, he related the story of the payroll robbery and the two surviving bandits to James Will and left town for good.

Neither Will nor most of Clifford's residents put much stock into the tale — until May 1931, when George Elkins found a stone inscribed "1847"; some words also seemed to be carved in the stone, but exposure to the elements had made them illegible. Treasure seekers dug far and wide but did not discover any cache — or the other two stones — in the area.

However, in November 1934, another stone was found by Tom Hatton. This stone read: "D. Grover and Joseph Fox-Lawe — Aug. 8, 1847." People assumed that these were the names of the two robbers, but more treasure hunting did not turn up the gold.

Although one of the robbers may have returned and found the money, many people believe that the stolen payroll is still buried near Clifford. According to author Perry Eberhart, who has written about the cache, a careful treasure hunter might find the metal pots containing a fortune in gold on one of the hills that lie east of Clifford.

56

Of course, anyone finding the treasure would be unable to keep it legally. But this hasn't stopped many treasure trackers from trying.

LAWS on CRIMINAL TREASURE

Stolen property belongs to the original owner, if there is proof connecting the property to the robbery. If someone finds the Clifford treasure, the U.S. Army would be able to claim the payroll legally as long as it could prove that the coins were part of that payroll. In one recent case, a boy in Cleveland, Ohio, who found close to $100,000 in currency buried in his backyard was not allowed to keep it because the serial numbers on the bills indicated that it had been part of the loot in a bank robbery; the money was returned to the bank.

Lost treasure, hidden treasure, criminal treasure: three types of treasure commonly hunted and found. Still other treasures — which many people never stop to consider — do exist. You'll read about them in the next chapter.

4. . . . And Three More

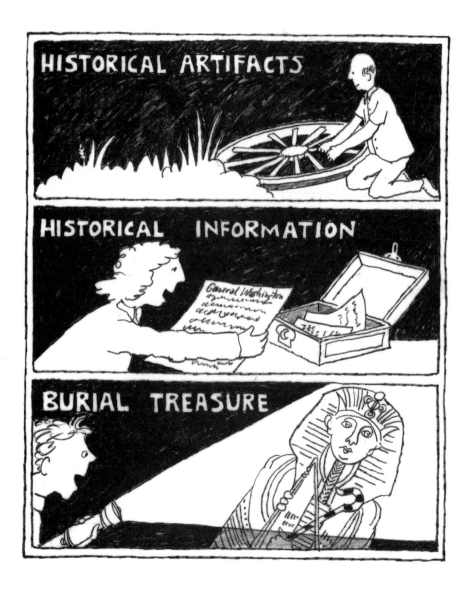

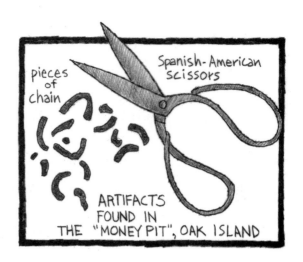

pieces of chain

Spanish-American scissors

ARTIFACTS FOUND IN THE "MONEY PIT", OAK ISLAND

Treasure Type 4: Historical artifacts

Some treasures are sought not for monetary worth but for historical value. A piece of history can be priceless, since it connects the hunter to the past. That's why some people search for *artifacts;* that is, old manmade objects that are not normally considered valuable. Usually, artifact hunters search in abandoned places where people lived and died — battlefields, ghost towns, old farmhouses, or building sites — for objects such as old bottles, belt buckles, and even buttons.

One artifact hunter, John D. Irwin, Jr., received a call one day from his friend Kurt Deppenschmit, who said that the field in back of his house had just been plowed. This was good news to Irwin since a freshly plowed field can reveal many treasures. What's more, Deppenschmit's house in Trenton, New Jersey, was built in the late 1700s and had been used as an inn after the Revolutionary War. The farmer's field had all the signs of a good place for historical artifacts.

The men asked for the farmer's permission before starting their hunt. Then they pulled out their metal detectors and got to work. Right away, Deppenschmit found a King George III halfpenny, a British coin minted in 1806–1807 and probably worth a little less than twenty dollars today. Then Irwin located an 1807 United States large cent, which could be worth a few

KING GEORGE III HALF-PENNY

U.S. LARGE CENT

hundred dollars if in excellent condition. But the important find that day was Irwin's: a brass button inscribed "Long Live the President." As an expert on artifacts, Irwin knew how to identify the button. He pored over a copy of Alphaeus H. Albert's book *Record of American Uniform and Historical Buttons,* and discovered that the button had been worn at George Washington's inauguration in 1789. What's more, only ten buttons of this kind were known to exist. Thanks to Irwin, an additional

60

inaugural button had been found. More important, the discovery encouraged him to read about Washington's inauguration and to speculate on how the button had become lost. That's the true sign of an artifact hunter: the history of the object becomes more important than the object's value. According to Irwin's research:

> The atmosphere following the Revolution was more relaxed, and the area north of Trenton would have probably provided an opportunity for Washington and his entourage of statesmen and generals to visit the campgrounds or headquarters within the vicinity. The scene would have been much like today's veterans visiting the beaches of Normandy [a French battle site in World War II] to reminisce and to thank those who showed them kindness during those trying times.

Irwin even tracked down Alphaeus H. Albert and shared his idea with him. Albert agreed that a visit by President Washington might well have precipitated the lost button.

LAWS on ARTIFACTS

Artifacts found on private property belong to the landowner, unless the landowner and the treasure tracker have a written agreement that indicates otherwise (see the Appendix for an example). Although artifact hunting on property belonging to the National Park Service is illegal, it is permissible on land belonging to the National Forest Service. In this case, any artifacts belong to the finder.

Treasure Type 5: Historical information

Some treasure trackers are more interested in discovering information about past events than in locating an actual object. Perhaps they want to explore a battlefield or the site of an old fort — not to recover a treasure, but to determine what exactly happened at these sites, especially if there's any controversy surrounding the historical events.

One such controversy pertains to the Donner tragedy. In mid-August 1846, when many pioneers were heading for California, a group of eighty-nine people known as the Donner Party chose to take a short cut in their journey. This decision, which required them to cut a thirty-six-mile road through Utah's Wasatch Mountains, would spell doom for almost half the emigrants.

In early September, as they crossed the eighty-mile-long flats of the Great Salt Lake Desert in Utah, most of their cattle and oxen died; wagons and possessions had to be abandoned; and men and women were forced to carry their young children. By the end of October, six of the emigrants had died. Still, most of the group managed to reach Truckee Lake, high in the Sierra Nevada Mountains of California. They tried to cross the mountain pass and reach Sutter's Fort before winter set in. But the disastrous short cut and desert crossing had delayed them too long; the snow was already three feet deep, so they stayed at Truckee Lake, where they found one cabin from a previous wagon train and built two others to shelter themselves from the winter.

The other members of the party, including the Donner family, had lagged behind and become separated from the main group. On November 3, they were forced to stop when a wagon axle broke at Alder Creek, about six miles from Truckee Lake (since renamed Donner Lake). There, they were only able to set up makeshift tents, using branches and animal skins, before a heavy snowfall blanketed them.

According to all accounts, those at Alder Creek suffered the most that winter, although a shortage of food and a lack of cooperation plagued both locations. At its worst, the snow was twenty-two feet deep, which only complicated the emigrants' desperate situation. Both groups were rescued eventually, but not before thirteen at Truckee Lake and nine at Alder Creek had died of starvation and exposure to the cold — and a few of the survivors had reportedly turned to cannibalism. Fourteen others died attempting to cross the mountain pass, leaving only forty-seven survivors to tell the story.

The Donner Trail has since been identified for its

historical significance. The Truckee Lake and Alder Creek campsites now belong to the National Forest Service and are part of the Donner Memorial State Park. Many people — treasure trackers and archaeologists alike — are fascinated by the Donner tragedy and the many legends that surround it.

Some are interested in tales of lost gold. It was rumored that some members of the party buried gold and jewels as they abandoned their wagons on the salt flats. Such an idea was begun by Virginia Reed, a young girl traveling with her family in the Donner Party. She asserted that one of the Reeds' wagons, named the Pioneer Palace, was buried along with many valuable possessions in the desert sand. During the 1980s, archaeologists Bruce Hawkins and David Madsen explored the site of the wagon burials and concluded that Virginia Reed had been mistaken. Wagons and household goods were buried, they discovered, but nothing of great value. In their explorations, the archaeologists found metal and wooden wagon parts, animal bones, and the charcoal residue from the pioneers' fires. They also found wagon ruts, most likely from the Pioneer Palace, almost 150 years after it set out for California.

Others are interested in studying the Donner Lake and Alder Creek campsites for historical information. For example, in April 1879, the Donner Lake cabin sites were informally excavated by some survivors and author C. F. McGlashan, who later wrote a book on the subject.

McGlashan noted that

> many of the leading citizens were present and assisted in searching for the relics. . . . A great many pins have been found, most of which are the old-fashioned round-headed ones. A strange feature in regard to these pins is that although bright and clean, they crumble and break at almost the slightest touch. . . . One of the most touching relics, in view of the sad, sad history, is the sole of an infant's shoe. The tiny babe who wore the shoe was probably among the number who perished of starvation.

A more recent excavation of the Alder Creek area took place during the summer of 1990. A group of archaeology professors and students from the University of Nevada in Reno, headed by Dr. Don Hardesty, explored the theory that the actual location of the tents at Alder Creek was misidentified. How could this have happened? First, fewer people survived that location. Second, their flimsy tents would have deteriorated quickly, leaving no permanent record. What's more, when Peter Wedell marked the Donner Lake and Alder Creek sites for historical purposes during the 1920s, he had to guess at the actual site of the Alder Creek tents. He based his decision on the location of some tall tree stumps and a partly burned ponderosa pine tree. The Donner Lake sites, on the other hand, were easily identified by the foundations of the three cabins.

Professor Hardesty wanted to set the record straight. What is interesting about his "treasure hunt" is that he was accompanied by a team of three treasure hunters, equipped with metal detectors. Although archaeologists and treasure hunters usually do not mix well, this time they teamed up to produce important results. First, the detectorists scanned the area with their machines. Every time they heard a signal, they placed a stickpin flag at that location. Then the archaeologists dug carefully at each flag location and removed any objects they found. When something important was uncovered, they placed it in a plastic bag and filled out forms about the location of the discovery.

During June and July 1990, the team covered the "official" tent sites at Alder Creek and found no remnants of the Donner families. Nearby, however, they turned up many artifacts, including tools, wagon parts, coins, china fragments, and upholstery tacks. Was this the real location of the Alder Creek tents? Even these artifacts cannot definitely prove that the Donners had camped at that site. According to William Lindemann, curator of the Emigrant Trail Museum at the Donner Memorial State Park, people are unaware that over a period of many years, moles and other rodents have a habit of moving and thereby scattering artifacts that have

been left behind. Pinpointing the location will take years of exacting study. Nonetheless, Professor Hardesty hopes to provide a conclusive result and, when that occurs, to request that the regional archaeologist of the National Forest Service correct the error. If that happens, Professor Hardesty will have found the treasure he sought: the correction of history.

In the meantime, should you wish to visit the Alder Creek site, take Route 89 north until you see the National Forest Service sign: Donner Camp Picnic Site. You will find two trails that form a loop through the site. To see the misidentified location, take the left-hand trail and follow the signs. To see Hardesty's location, take the right-hand trail and, as the trail curves to the left, look for the small area of broken ground on the left. A few clumps of dirt may not look important, but the artifacts they reveal may change a small piece of history.

LAWS on HISTORICAL INFORMATION

Anyone can search for historical information in libraries. However, treasure trackers and archaeologists must get special permission to search historical sites. They are generally not permitted to keep anything they find; after study, it is turned over to the government or the association in charge of the site. Even removing a stone from a site can lead to a lawsuit and mar the study of history.

Treasure Type 6: Burial treasure

Treasure hunters are sometimes called grave robbers, because some treasures can be found in grave sites. A respectable person would never dig for treasure in a cemetery, but what about burial places — like pyramids or other tombs — where rulers or well-to-do people were buried by the citizens of ancient civilizations?

Treasures found in such places are usually located not by treasure hunters but by archaeologists. One excavation that revealed great treasures was conducted at Mancheng, China, in 1968. Some Chinese soldiers noticed a strange land formation, often a sign of a buried archaeological site. These soldiers had discovered the 2,000-year-old tombs of Prince Liu Sheng and his wife, Prin-

68

cess Dou Wan. The tombs had been constructed during their lifetime to be ready when the royal couple died. After their deaths, the tombs were sealed with heavy stones. Then iron was melted at the site and poured over the stones, so that the outside world would be prevented from intruding.

The soldiers communicated their discovery to their superiors; soon after, archaeologists from Peking visited the site to begin their work. Inside one tomb, they found a main chamber and three smaller ones. In one of the small chambers were the remains of several chariots and the skeletons of twelve horses. Food and wine had been stored in large jars in the second small chamber. But the exciting discovery was a jumbled heap of what looked like jade tablets. When one archaeologist examined a tablet, however, he saw that it was connected to the others by tiny threads. In fact, the tablets had been drilled at each corner and then sewn with gold thread into a jade burial suit. Another suit was found in the second tomb. Ancient Chinese believed that jade could preserve a body from decay. Although historical documents indicated that jade suits had been used, none had ever been found — until the discovery of Liu Sheng's and Dou Wan's tombs.

Archaeologists studied the suits with care. Each was composed of twelve sections, including shoes and gloves. Liu Sheng's suit was made of almost 2,700 pieces of jade, while Dou Wan's had almost 2,200. Because

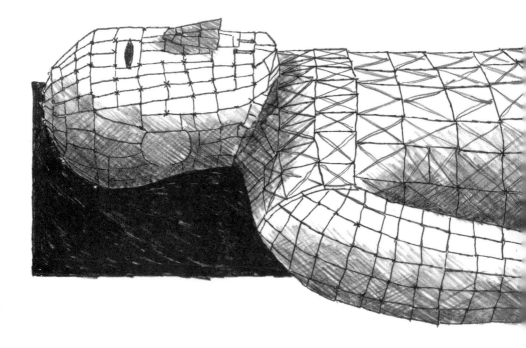

of the intricate nature of the suits, some archaeologists estimated that it took as long as ten years to make them. These treasures are now displayed at the Peking Palace Museum.

LAWS on BURIAL TREASURE

If you happen to come across the site of a lost civilization, proceed no farther. There are federal rules and regulations that prohibit the excavation of any archaeological site. Report your discovery to the proper authorities and hope that your name will go down in history books. That would be the best reward.

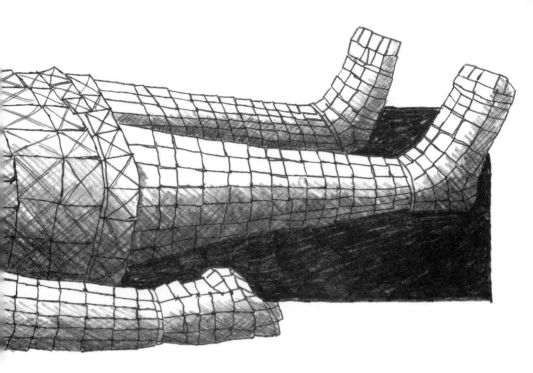

These six types of treasure are the most common kinds that people hunt. But finding one is no simple task. You'll need to decide upon a tracking technique which may require special equipment. The next chapter will show you how.

5. Treasure-Tracking Techniques

By now you're probably wondering how people locate treasures. In this chapter, you'll learn six of the techniques they use.

Method 1: Detecting metal

The most common way to find buried metallic treasure is with a metal detector. This machine resembles a pie plate attached to a broomstick; the tip of the broomstick contains a control box that gives audible signals when the pie plate passes over metal. It may look strange, but it can locate valuable metal items, such as coins and jewelry, that are not otherwise visible. It can also locate pull tabs from soda cans and bottle caps. A treasure tracker must be able to use the detector skillfully. For example, you can set your machine to detect only silver coins or gold rings. When the detector encounters one of these objects, it gives off a certain sound. This sound can be quite faint, which explains why many detectorists wear headphones; they want to hear every beep and ping their machine makes. After a while, a detectorist will know exactly what he or she has found by the sound alone.

Metal detectors come in different sizes, strengths, and prices. They are available in toy stores for under $30 and in treasure-hunting stores for anywhere from $150 to well over $500. Although you may be able to find some treasures with a toy-store machine, you'll increase your odds if you can afford even the least expensive adult model.

Metal detectors are probably most used by individuals searching for coins and jewelry. But they can be used to search for gold nuggets, too. One gold hunter was Floyd Allen. After receiving a tip, he drove to a destination in the middle of the desert and turned on his new detector. At first, as he scanned the side of a canyon, he uncovered only scraps of wire and lead. Then he heard a new sound—"waaaamp"—which Allen described as "a nice,

soft, sweet sound, so I figured it was more lead." Happily, it turned out to be a gold nugget. Since that time, Allen has worked the area frequently, uncovering more than fifteen nuggets. Although he has written about his gold-hunting experiences, he has not revealed any clues to the site or even the state in which it is located. He obviously wants to continue his search alone.

Method 2: Beachcombing

A much less expensive method—if you live near a beach, lake, or pond — is beachcombing. Although a beachcomber can use a metal detector, many use only

water scoop

their eyes and a water scoop, which is available at treasure-hunting supply stores.

One beachcomber, William Longo, has practiced his treasure-tracking talents in many places across the United States. Longo is especially interested in fossil hunting in and along beachfronts. Once he had waded seventy yards into the waist-deep water of Chesapeake Bay when he scooped up an arrowhead. Archaeologists told him that it was made by a Native American almost 3,000 years ago, when the Chesapeake Bay shoreline was quite different. Longo has also scooped up a recently minted penny and a 20,000,000-year-old shark's tooth at the same time.

Most beachcombers know that the best time to explore a beach is after a storm at low tide — in winter, when few people are on the beach. A clever beachcomber will learn to identify spots where the waves tend to deposit heavier objects. Coins are often found in groups, sifted together in the sand. Beachcombers also take note where most people congregate during the summer months — spots that are likely to reveal missing treasure. Finally, beachcombers know that they must also wade into the water. Shallow water can lead to many jewelry discoveries — since rings often slip off fingers that contract in cold water.

Method 3: Visual searching

Certain treasures can be found just by using your eyes. For example, arrowheads are easy to locate; they're prized by treasure hunters interested in the history of Native Americans. Once you know where to look, you can find them in almost every part of the United States. The only tool you need is a "hunting stick," which can be a broom handle or even a branch used to poke through debris on the ground.

Leon Gilmore of Tulsa, Oklahoma, has collected more than 40,000 arrowheads, according to writer Tom Vance. The collection includes spear points dated from 8000 to 10,000 B.C. and arrowheads from the 1800s. Gilmore, who is part Cherokee Indian, attributes his large collection to the fact that he's "interested in Indian history and culture. I used to visit my grandmother on her farm in Claremore, Oklahoma. I got started in collecting early by picking up arrowheads and I just never lost interest through the years."

Phillip Sisco, another arrowhead collector of Cherokee ancestry, says that "it's a thrill to find something made by another, earlier human being and so long ago. It's the feeling that I have something that was made way back in history. I actually have history in my hands."

"hunting stick"

Where do you look for arrowheads? It's a good idea to read about the history of local tribes before you begin. Ideally, you'll want to know where their campsites were and which trails they followed. Even if you can't locate this type of information, you may still have some luck. C. G. Yeager, the author of a guidebook to hunting arrowheads, advises a hunter to look for high ground, where campgrounds might have been. Riverbanks, he writes, are not good locations for arrowheads. Since Native Americans were well aware that rivers flooded in the spring, they set up camps farther away.

Other times, you may want to do a visual search even though you don't know exactly what you'll find. Here are three places to consider.

Fence posts. One uncommon treasure site is found beneath old fence posts, especially in rural areas. People often buried their money, rather than depositing it in banks, because they wanted to be able to retrieve it quickly. For this reason, many people hid money in "posthole banks."

A posthole is the hole into which a fence post is placed. The posts are then connected by barbed wire.

A "bank" was made by hollowing out a space beneath one fence post so that a container of valuables could be placed there. That way, when the depositor wanted to recover the money, he or she simply lifted the post out of the ground and reclaimed it.

A field can have hundreds of fence posts surrounding it. How do you find the right posthole? Angie Irons, who has researched the subject, has some suggestions. First, find an old farm with a cooperative landowner; be sure to complete a search agreement (see the Appendix). In some cases, the farmhouse may no longer be standing, although its fences still are. Second, stand at a fence post and look down the row of posts, searching for anything unusual. Notice any posts that seem higher or lower or more out of line than the others. Look for any barbed wire that seems loosely attached to a post. Third, inspect each post for markings. Posts that hid treasure caches were often notched or marked in some way. Some even had horseshoes nailed to them. Finally, you may want to use a metal detector to determine whether you've found a hidden bank before you start digging — but a visual search may be just as effective.

According to Irons, farmers in Oklahoma, Texas, Arkansas, and New Mexico were especially likely to use such a banking system. Most posthole banks will not make you wealthy. If you want to find one, remember that the container holding the money — even if it's a Mason jar — may be valuable, too. So dig carefully.

Drainage systems. Stan Lang, of Cheyenne, Wyoming, owned an ice cream parlor situated next to a car wash. At closing time one night, a teenager burst into the parlor and asked Stan how to find the car wash owner. Apparently, he had just washed his ring into the drain.

This mishap gave Stan an idea: car wash drains might hold many treasures. As people wash their cars, their hands become slippery and cold, and jewelry or money can easily be lost. He quickly became an expert on car wash treasures.

He discovered that the drainage systems in most car washes collect water in a trap. Then the sludge is cleaned out and removed, sometimes to the town dump, sometimes to a nearby lot. Stan began to ask car wash owners for permission to search their sludge dumps — not an idea that will appeal to everyone.

Garage sales. One of the easiest places to find treasure is perhaps the most overlooked. J. P. Miller walked out of his house one cold March day and saw a yard sale down the street. Although he wasn't usually inclined to shop at yard sales, he decided to stop anyway. Being a curious kind of guy, Miller saw a cardboard box that looked interesting. In it, there were some pairs of used work gloves, which he thought he might be able to use. He paid fifty cents for the gloves. At home, as he was checking to see if each glove had its mate, he felt something hard inside one. He turned the glove upside-down; out fell a plastic bag containing forty-five coins. The coins included thirty-two Indian head pennies dated 1880 to 1907 and four Liberty Head nickels dated 1883 to 1907. Miller's experience shows that treasure can be hiding in strange and unexpected places.

The best buy at a garage sale may be an unsorted box of junk or a locked chest. Many people who clean out their attics or garages simply want to get rid of their old possessions; they never stop to consider that they might own some treasure.

Method 4: Dowsing

One of the most unusual ways of hunting treasure is dowsing. There are two variations of this technique: one is intended for armchair treasure trackers, the other for those already out in the field.

The armchair technique, called *remote dowsing*, involves a large-scale map of the suggested treasure site and a pendulum. Usually a detailed road map or, even better, a topographical map (which shows land formations as well as roads) will suffice. The dowser must be totally relaxed and have nothing else in mind. Then the dowser visualizes the suspected treasure: a gold mine, coins, belt buckles, bottles, whatever.

The dowser then takes a pendulum, made by tying a piece of thread or string to a ring, and holds it over the map. The dowser moves his or her arm back and forth across the map — very slowly — so as not to cause the pendulum to swing. If the pendulum begins to swing, the dowser notes the exact spot on the map over which the swinging began. This is the site of the treasure. According to many dowsers, the more the pendulum swings, the bigger the treasure.

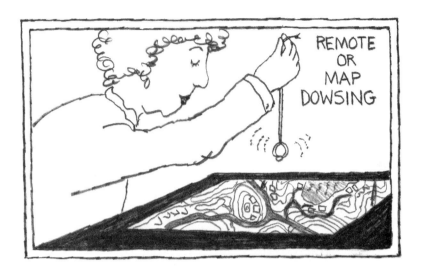

REMOTE OR MAP DOWSING

The other version of dowsing, called *site dowsing,* involves the use of a forked stick. The dowser holds the stick by the ends and, visualizing the treasure, carries it in front while walking across the area of the suspected treasure. If treasure is present, the stick will point toward the earth at the correct site. This technique is also used to find water — and has been employed with great success.

Are you suspicious of such a treasure-hunting technique? Reg Smith of Danville, Vermont, certainly became a believer. One day in 1958, he and Clint Gray were cutting wood when he noticed that his wrist watch was gone. The undergrowth was so heavy in the area that Smith was almost certain he would never find it.

Gray, however, was an experienced dowser and thought he had a chance to find the watch. He made a forked stick and, picturing the watch in his mind, walked through the area where they had been cutting wood. The stick bent down once, but the men could not find the watch at this spot. Gray tried again — and despite the fact that he walked all over the site, the stick bent again at the same spot. A second search did not reveal the watch.

The next day, after a night of heavy rain, the men came back to cut more wood. As a lark, they checked the spot that the dowsing rod had indicated twice. There was the watch, sticking out of the ground. The rain had washed it from its muddy hiding place.

Method 5: Puzzle solving

Some people are more interested in solving treasure mysteries with brainpower than with metal detectors or other equipment. These hunters look for codes that, when deciphered, will lead to hidden fortunes, such as Beale's and the Buzzard's treasures. Unfortunately, not many authentic treasure codes exist. For this reason, many puzzles have been invented over the years to test the minds of treasure trackers.

84

Usually, a company buries a valuable object at a secret location and advertises a treasure-tracking contest. If you send in some money, you will receive a sheet of clues written in complex code which will supposedly lead you to the treasure. Sometimes the buried treasure is worth a great deal of money and sometimes it is not. What sounds like fun at first can quickly become frustrating. And the only one likely to become richer is the company sponsoring the hunt.

One famous puzzle was devised by author-illustrator Kit Williams. In 1980, Williams published a children's book entitled *Masquerade,* which contained illustrated and written clues that when solved would reveal the spot where a golden hare could be found. Many people bought the book for its beautiful pictures; others purchased it because they wanted to find the treasure.

As it happened, the person who discovered the golden hare did not even bother to solve the puzzle. Instead, this treasure hunter used a clever tactic: he researched the life of Kit Williams rather than spending time deciphering the code. Once he knew where Williams had lived as a young boy and where his favorite childhood haunts were, he traveled there in search of the golden hare. Luckily for him, he stumbled upon a stone monument which led him to the treasure.

Such an approach may take the fun out of puzzle solving, but it also points out the problems with some manufactured treasure hunts: they are only as good as the imagination of the person inventing the puzzle. Kit Williams obviously did not spend enough time choosing a good hiding spot.

The developers of another treasure hunt learned many lessons from Williams's example, especially when it came to hiding their treasure. They made sure that the burial location had nothing to do with their lives. But they also made their puzzle too complex and confusing.

In 1984, the Golden Horse Treasure Hunt was announced. In that contest, treasure hunters could purchase a book (entitled *Treasure*, by Sheldon Renan), a videotape, and a laser disk. All three contained clues to the location of a golden horse, made of 2.2 pounds of solid gold and hidden somewhere in the United States. The person who discovered the horse would get to keep it and would also receive $25,000 a year for twenty years.

The golden horse had to be found by May 26, 1989. More than 75,000 people bought the book and 15,000 videos were sold during the span of the contest. Some people spent almost $100 on all three items.

Even schoolchildren joined in the hunt. The fourth- and fifth-grade classes at the Elizabeth Ann Seton School in Lakeland, New York, arranged to meet with the puzzle maker, who called himself Dr. Crypton (he is officially known as Paul Hoffman). They didn't get any answers, but the children were inspired to work on the solution. Two fifth graders eventually deciphered two important clues that helped the children determine in which state the horse was buried.

But the puzzle was so intricate that decoding two clues was not enough to lead them to the golden horse. Many others also thought they had solved the puzzle, but the only way to verify their solution was to visit the location of the golden horse — and start digging. More than a few people made pilgrimages to the site they thought contained the treasure, at great expense.

Writer Brad Jolley shared many stories of the thwarted hunters in an article in *Treasure* magazine. Helen Kerchner, who lives in Indiana, visited Tennessee once and Utah twelve times. One angry contestant told Jolley that she had lost her job and her marriage because of the puzzle. As she put it,

I was one of those people who got swept up in Golden Horse fever. I was obsessed! . . . Every waking moment I spent either working on that thing or thinking about it. . . . I spent thousands of dollars travelling to Oregon. . . . I prayed for the day I would finally be free of this thing that had taken away my normal life. . . . I bought all the versions of the puzzle. I almost wore out my VCR watching that video so many times . . . I learned Japanese. I learned Greek. I studied maps. . . . The puzzle was like a dog trying to catch its own tail. Just when you thought you were getting close to catching it, it was just out of reach.

It wasn't the money that attracted me. . . . It was the fact that I consider myself to be an intelligent being, and if another human being designed this, then I [should] be able to figure it out.

Despite everyone's best efforts, no one found the horse by the contest deadline. In August 1989, the horse was retrieved from its place of burial and donated, along with $500,000, to the Big Brothers and Big Sisters of America. Thousands of treasure hunters were sorely disappointed. The contest organizers wouldn't even tell them where the horse had been buried or what the solution to the puzzle was.

One treasure hunter managed to solve the puzzle, a few months after the deadline. His story, which appeared in the March 1990 issue of *Treasure,* reveals his solution to the puzzle. It was tricky for a number of reasons. First, the book and the videos were filled with many small visual clues. Second, a message written in secret code required the solution of four different clues by using three different ciphers. Finally, even with the message deciphered, the exact location of the horse was difficult to determine — unless other clues were solved along the way.

A very clever puzzle cost thousands of people a lot of money and hard work. If you want to try your hand at it, you may be able to find a copy of Renan's book at your local library. If and when you give up, you can check the solution in *Treasure* magazine.

Method 6: Dreaming

Some people dream about finding a fortune; others have dreams that lead them to riches. One person who paid attention to his dreams was Alonso Fletcher, who lived near Gallipolis, Ohio. One night in early October 1904, Fletcher dreamed that he had discovered a gold mine on the farm of a neighbor named Thomas McCormick. The next night, he had the same dream. This time it was even more vivid and so lifelike that he could see the exact spot where the gold mine was supposed to be.

The following morning, he visited McCormick's farm and found the spot he had dreamed about. He dug into the ground and uncovered a vein of strange-looking ore, which he sent to Salt Lake City to be assayed. The ore turned out to be part iron and part gold. Fletcher's dream had come true, but he did not pursue the mine, according to the Columbus *Dispatch*. Perhaps McCormick didn't want to share the mine with anyone.

You may want to keep a record of your dreams, just in case a treasure appears while you're sleeping.

Now that you've read about six techniques for tracking treasure, you can decide which one suits you best. But you can't pick your method until you know what you want to hunt for, and you can't start hunting until you've completed the most important step of all, as you'll discover in the next two chapters.

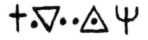

89

Part II.
Becoming a Treasure Tracker

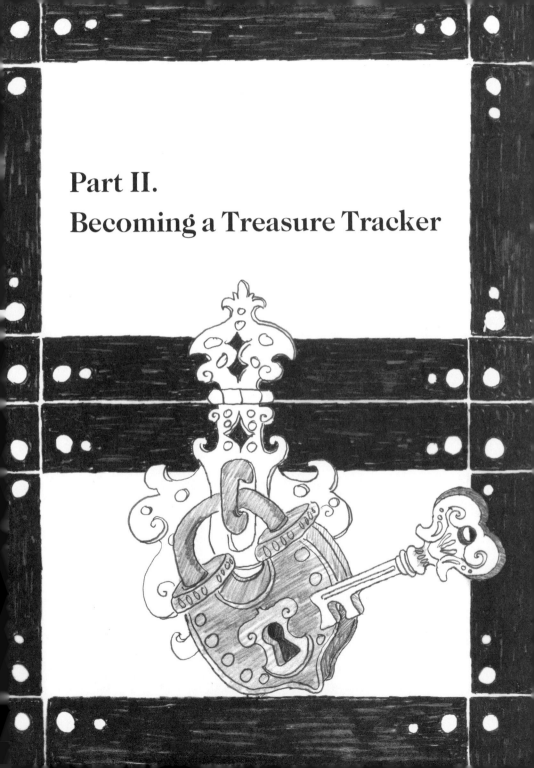

6. Beginning Your Treasure Hunt

The first step in starting a treasure hunt is to visit your local library. There you will find information about people who have located treasures in your area. You will also be able to read about treasures that remain to be discovered in your state. What's more, you should find some clues to good treasure-tracking areas in your vicinity. Experienced treasure trackers know that thorough library research will help them locate a treasure.

What should you do when you walk into your library?

Library Tip 1: Know what you want to look for

The most successful treasure hunters don't try to find everything; instead they become specialists. By concentrating your search, you will develop expert knowledge of one or two treasures and the best places to find them. What's more, if you focus on a local treasure, you will spend a lot less time and money traveling to distant treasure sites.

If you're not sure about what you want to find, you can read books on the general topic of "treasure hunting" or "treasure-trove." You'll be able to locate these in the library's subject catalog.

Library Tip 2: Locate treasure information

Most people automatically assume that books are the best source of information, but this is not true. Most books about treasure are less likely to be of value than other sources. Why? Treasure books usually contain fanciful stories which, though entertaining, don't provide enough information for the serious tracker.

Two better sources of treasure information are treasure magazines and microfilms.

Treasure magazines. Monthly treasure magazines contain up-to-date articles about lost treasures as well as advertisements for the latest books on treasure hunting. Reading the current issue won't help you much, unless you get lucky and find a story about a missing local treasure. To have a better chance, you'll need to read the

back issues of the magazine which are stored in the library. These are bound and either shelved with the regular books or stored in an area reserved for librarians.

If your library does not subscribe to any, you can start your own subscription. Three magazines you may want to consider are:

Lost Treasure, P.O. Box 1589, Grove, Oklahoma 74344;

Treasure, 1111 Rancho Conejo Blvd., Suite 105, Newbury Park, California 91320;

Western & Eastern Treasures, P.O. Box 253, Mt. Morris, Illinois 61054.

Newspaper microfilms. Old newspapers are another good source of treasure information. Since newsprint becomes brittle and deteriorates over time and since most libraries cannot store large stacks of old newspapers, many have been put on microfilm. Your town may have several local papers, especially from one hundred or more years ago. You may want to do some exploring on the microfilm machine.

If this sounds as though it might take a long time, you're right. But old newspapers were shorter than today's; in fact, most had no more than ten pages and were filled with many advertisements. A true treasure tracker will explore old newspapers, no matter how difficult this may seem.

Library Tip 3: Discover your library's other resources

Besides books, magazines,and newspapers, your library may have two other special resources.

Local-history collection. This is often housed in a separate room or area of the library and contains reading material of local or regional interest. Such a collection may include books written about specific treasures in your state. These books will usually have more detailed information which should help a serious tracker. The collection could also include special files on local treasure stories or legends. If you become skillful at using local-history material, you're well on your way to finding treasure.

Oral history collection. One often overlooked source of treasure information is the oral history. Oral histories are interviews in which people recount the story of their lives. The interviews are tape-recorded and then usually transcribed. Many libraries have small collections of the oral histories of past local residents. Sometimes these are shelved in the local history collection.

For example, the University of New Mexico Library contains a collection of oral histories from the Pioneers Foundation. One man who was interviewed numerous times about his past was Jack Stockbridge; he never went to school and didn't learn to read or write until he was an adult. Despite this, he was a soldier in the Spanish-American War, where he rode alongside Teddy Roosevelt. Eventually, he became a prospector. As Lou Blachly, his interviewer, said of Stockbridge: "He has . . . witnessed more deeds of violence and more killings and deaths than any person I have recorded. But the most phenomenal thing of all about Jack is that memory of his."

One of his memories concerned a hidden cache of stolen gold. A bandit named Jimmy Burns stole about $5,000 in gold from a saloon in Silver City, New Mexico, and got on a stagecoach headed for Globe, Arizona. A little way from town on the Lordsburg Flats, Burns realized he might be picked up on the other end, so he told the driver to stop the stage. Then he buried the gold next to a yucca plant, into which he stuck a gun as a landmark. Shortly after reaching Globe, Burns died. No one has ever found the gold.

Stockbridge remembered the probable location, which provides a tip for anyone interested in finding the cache of gold: the old stagecoach road from Silver City to Globe, right before a cutoff, where the stagecoach changed horses. Stockbridge told Blachly:

> The old road used to . . . come out through by Tyrone and come in by the Terrin place and . . . by the Knight place and around that way. Well, they later made a cutoff, made a road to benefit these people here along the river here to go to Silver City and went . . . up Echo Canyon and went down through . . . Wind Canyon on into Silver City . . . used to come right through Duncan.

An old map and a metal detector might help someone locate the gold Jack Stockbridge remembered.

Library Tip 4: Talk to your librarian

If you can't find any material, don't hesitate to discuss your needs with a librarian. Explain that you're a serious treasure tracker and that you're looking for information. If you describe exactly what type of material you want, your librarian should be able to help you. In some cases, your librarian may be able to request material from a larger library.

If all else fails, ask if your library has or can borrow a copy of Robert F. Marx's book *Buried Treasure of the United States*. This book lists treasures still to be found

in the United States, including the District of Columbia. Marx gives basic information; the rest is up to the serious treasure tracker to research. This information, though, may help your librarian steer you in the right direction.

Remember not to ask for the impossible. If you live in North Dakota, it won't do much good to ask where you can find local pirate treasure. That's an easier question for a Florida librarian. Remember, too, that although the librarian will help you find material, the reading and thinking are up to you.

7. Five Clues to Consider

Finding treasure information in the library is only the first part of your library search. Once you have found magazines or newspapers to read, you'll need to look for clues to treasure sites. Although there are many sites to consider, five favorites are listed below.

If you're going to become a serious treasure tracker, you will need to keep a record of the material you read and the leads you encounter. An index-card system is probably best, according to treasure researcher Dick Stout. Keep an index-card file with headings of possible treasure sites: Ghost Towns, Trails, Parks, Old Schools, and so on. Every time you find something useful, record it on a card, along with the title and date of the magazine or newspaper, or the title and author of the book, and file it in your card box. Once you move your treasure hunt outdoors, you may want to refer to your reading material for other clues.

Site Clue 1: Ghost towns

Many people make the mistake of picturing tumble-weeds and desert landscapes when they think about ghost towns. Although most ghost towns are found in the western United States, every state has them. A ghost town is simply a deserted settlement. It may contain actual buildings or just remnants of their foundations; in some cases, every trace of the town may have vanished — except, of course, its buried treasure.

In 1938, according to historical researcher Donald Viles, Jacksonville, Oregon, was almost a ghost town. Once it had been a thriving gold mine town. But in 1938, only three businesses remained open; every other building along the dirt road that served as the main street was deserted.

One day that summer three young boys, Robert and Edward Lewis and Arthur Jefferson, decided to explore an abandoned building. This was an activity that they enjoyed; in fact, they had explored almost every old building in town, except a small one that had never looked interesting. What the boys didn't know is that

102

the building used to be the Beekman Bank, where many miners had deposited their money. When the mines ran out in 1902, the bank closed for business.

The boys soon discovered an unlocked rear door and in a moment they were in the bank. Since the bank had not been used for more than thirty years, everything was covered with dust. They found old newspapers and envelopes that seemed to be stuffed full. They ripped open the envelopes and found enough gold and silver coins to fill a bank money bag.

The boys had never seen this much money. They knew they were rich, so they divided the coins and made some plans. First, they would treat themselves to candy and ice cream. Second, each boy would take two handfuls of the larger coins and hide them in the town. Third, the rest of the coins would be buried in the Lewis brothers' backyard. Finally, each boy would keep a silver dollar to give to his mother.

If the store owner wondered where the boys got the money to treat themselves, he said nothing. No one noticed the boys as they hid their handfuls of coins in the walls of one of the town buildings. They even managed to bury the money bag in the Lewis backyard without being detected. But when their sons handed them the silver dollars the mothers became suspicious.

"Where did you get these?" they asked.

The boys quickly made up a story about earning the money, but the two women had heard enough. They escorted their sons to the town marshal, who managed to scare the boys into telling *almost* everything. They explained how they had found the money, where they had spent it, and where they had buried the bag of coins. They told about everything except the two handfuls of coins that each had secreted in the deserted building.

They were so scared by their encounter with the law they never went back to the building to reclaim their coins. Eventually, the Lewis brothers and Arthur Jefferson moved away. As far as they know, none of the coins was ever found.

Treasure Hint

As you read old newspapers or treasure magazines, be on the lookout for any mention of ghost towns in your area. If you don't come across any, ask your librarian if there are any maps of your general area from the 1800s. A careful comparison of an old map with a modern one may reveal that some towns no longer appear on the map. You may also want to contact (or even join) a local historical society, which should know of nearby ghost towns. Once you locate a ghost town, remember that one of the best spots to search is the old town dump. Every town had to dispose of its trash, and some of that refuse may now be quite valuable.

Site Clue 2: Transportation routes

Roads, foot trails, and even canal paths make good hunting spots for treasure. Travelers occasionally lost or discarded items along the way. Sometimes they even buried valuable possessions if they were in danger of being robbed. In some cases, the routes themselves may be constructed of hidden treasure.

One person who had a good deal of luck walking home from school along a gravel road was David Orchard of Glen Innes, Australia. He stubbed his toe on an enormous uncut blue sapphire, worth about $375,000 according to one estimate. David found the sapphire because a local mining company wanted to get rid of some of its waste rock and dirt and offered the slag to local residents for road improvements. Obviously, the mining company had missed the sapphire.

A more common type of road treasure was discovered by Richard Martin. Driving down a back road in Ohio one Sunday morning, he passed through a small town and noticed an intersection where three roads converged to create a small grassy triangle. He grabbed his metal detector and walked through the triangle in a methodical way. His detector found two Mercury dimes and a quarter, all of which were old enough to have been minted of silver. Another day, he spotted another triangular strip in another small town. Again his metal detector uncovered some treasures: six silver dimes, a child's silver ring, and four wheaties (pennies that have curved stalks of wheat on the back).

Still another type of road, popular at one point, was the wagon-train trail. Treasure hunter Tom Molnar wanted to find Rabbit Hole Springs, a Nevada campsite along the Applegate Trail. This trail was forged by Jesse Applegate after pioneers wanted another, easier route to reach Oregon. At one point, in August 1846, Applegate and his party had run short of water. Desperate to find some, he noticed rabbit tracks that he thought might lead them to a watering hole. The meager, brackish spring they found was justifiably named for the rabbits.

Unfortunately, this section of the Applegate Trail wasn't much better than the Donners' route. One wagon train, the Washington City Company, led by J. Goldsborough Bruff, found a most disturbing sight at Rabbit Hole Springs, according to author George R. Stewart.

> Emigrants had dug a number of wells . . . three to six feet deep and four or five feet across. Water had oozed in, clear and cool, but a little brackish, about half filling the holes. Unfortunately, half-dead oxen had a habit of wandering around, trying to drink at the wells, falling in head first, and drowning. Bruff saw four of the wells thus choked up, the carcasses swelled so as to fit the holes tightly, only the hindquarters and tails showing above the ground. All the ground in the vicinity was littered with carcasses. Though the stench was almost unbearable, Bruff conscientiously counted a dead mule, two dead horses, and eighty-two dead oxen. In addition, there were several lame and abandoned oxen, the wreck of one wagon, fragments of others, and the grave of a fifty-year-old man from Ohio.

The area around Rabbit Hole Springs could have held a number of treasures. But when Molnar and his partner spent three days there, they found nothing of interest. One day as they drove down the road, they tried to imagine what the area looked like almost 150 years ago. It was then that they noticed two faint tracks (that is, a trail) leading west in the direction of Black Rock, the next campsite on the Applegate Trail. They stopped and considered the tracks; they were certain they had stumbled across the original wagon trail.

They drove up the trail a short distance and parked their truck. Then they turned on their metal detectors and began to explore. Five minutes later, Molnar, who was standing over one of the wagon wheel tracks, heard a loud signal as he made his one and only find.

The earth was so hard that when he used his trowel, it came up in chunks. He broke the dirt apart and discovered a coin. In the middle of nowhere, on an old wagon-train trail, he had found an 1819 one-cent coin that was as large as a half dollar. It was well worn and worth maybe five dollars. But its history — and the surprise of finding it at all — was far more important.

That night, sitting in front of a campfire, Molnar wondered how the coin had been lost there.

Did it fall out of some little boy's or girl's pocket as they walked along beside the wagon? Or was that too much money for a child to have in those days? Maybe it was . . . in a wagon and it bounced out along the bumpy trail. Or was there a fight and it fell out during the skirmish?

Bobby Barnes, a Civil War relic hunter from Henderson, Tennessee, had his most fascinating day as a treasure hunter when he explored an old roadbed in Tennessee. Confederate troops, in retreat from the Battle of Shiloh, used the road that led to Corinth, Mississippi.

In November 1982, Barnes and some friends hunted along the road and uncovered a few pennies and buttons. Then Barnes turned his metal detector to the bank that lined the road. Within ten minutes he had found a rusty horseshoe. Disappointed, he heard the same sound from his detector a few moments later. Expecting to find another horseshoe, he dug three inches or so and saw something green, a sign that he had found a brass or copper item. He dug farther and pulled out a short artillery sword, worth perhaps $250. Other than the easily removed green tarnish, the sword was in perfect condition.

Treasure Hint

Look for mentions of transportation routes in old issues of your local newspaper. The older the road, the more likely you are to find treasure there, so steer clear of expressways and highways. The best road hunting may be found along old trails like the Oregon Trail (Missouri to Oregon) and the Natchez Trace Trail (Mississippi to Tennessee), less well known wagon-train trails such as the Applegate Trail, and even stagecoach trails. Old canal routes, such as the Erie Canal, which crisscrossed the mid-Atlantic states, can be found on maps; sites where locks and tollhouses existed are good hunting grounds. Old railroad lines, especially around the sites of railroad stations, may also yield treasures.

Site Clue 3: Public places

Anywhere people congregate is a good place to hunt for treasure. The trick is to find sites that are no longer meeting spots and where the treasures may be older. These include parks, bandstands, campgrounds, school-yards, drive-in theaters, amusement parks, and fair-grounds.

According to author Robert Marx, a member of the Houston Treasure and Relic Hunters Club read in an old newspaper that Houston's Memorial Park had been a military base during World War I. In fact, more than 30,000 soldiers had been stationed at Camp Logan and 185 buildings had stood in what is now a public park. This shrewd treasure hunter located a map of the former base which showed the exact location of the buildings; none of these existed any longer. Then he applied for permission from the city to search the area with the treasure club.

What did they find? For more than two years, club members spent weekends searching the park with metal detectors. During their search, they uncovered large quantities of bottles, buttons, coins, and watches, among other artifacts.

110

Two other hunters, David Hiott and Joe Allen, decided to have a look at one of the oldest areas of McPherson Park in Greenville, South Carolina. They used their metal detectors to explore an old duck pond, now drained, which had been a popular spot for picnickers who tossed coins into it for good luck.

Of course, they found some fishing sinkers, but they also discovered a great many pennies, dated as early as 1910, and one 1917 silver quarter. Near the end of the day, they stopped to investigate the area around an old barbecue. To his surprise, Hiott uncovered an 1875 Seated Liberty dime.

Treasure Hint

A thorough search of old local newspapers should give you an idea of public places that were once popular. When you have a list, you may be able to find their locations on old city maps or through interviews with older citizens. It is also worth checking places that still exist. Remember that a public place may look quite different from the way it did fifty to one hundred years ago, as was the case with the Houston park. Bandstands were once a popular feature of some parks, but they have often been torn down or fallen into disuse. Such a site might be worth a try. Another good location is a beach that used to have a bathhouse; if you can locate the site of the old bathhouse (usually indicated on old maps), you may be able to uncover coins with the use of a scoop and/or metal detector.

Site Clue 4: Robbers' caches

A cache (pronounced "cash") is a hiding place.

Reports of old robberies provide a good source for money that is still missing. Many robbers stole money only to become separated from it later. Be careful, though: once you have read a newspaper article about a robbery, make sure you continue your newspaper search. The money may have been found years later; you won't want to waste your time looking for a cache that has already been discovered. And you might not want to bother with one that you'll have to turn over to the police.

One of the most daring robberies of the twentieth century began as a skyjacking. On November 24, 1971, a man who called himself Dan Cooper purchased a one-way ticket from Portland, Oregon, to Seattle, Washington. Once he was on board Northwest Airlines Flight 305, he handed flight attendant Florence Schaffner a note that read: "Have bomb in briefcase. Will use it if necessary. Sit beside me. You are being hijacked."

112

Cooper then opened his briefcase, revealing what Schaffner thought were eight sticks of dynamite. During the flight to Seattle, Schaffner relayed messages to the cockpit of the Boeing 727. Cooper demanded $200,000 in used bills, which were to be placed in a knapsack. The knapsack and two parachutes were to be brought on board when the plane landed in Seattle. Cooper promised that the passengers would be released once the money and the parachutes were delivered.

Cooper set a deadline of 5 P.M., which gave the airline exactly one hour and forty minutes to locate $200,000 and deliver it to the airport. Since it was late in the day, this might have proved to be a problem; but the Seattle First National Bank kept $240,000 in a special fund reserved to pay off kidnappers. FBI agents, who had been called by the police, picked up the money and took it to the Seattle airport.

The twenty-pound bag of money and the parachutes were taken on board and inspected by Cooper. Once he was satisfied that everything was in order, he released all the passengers and two of the flight attendants. The remainder of the flight crew remained on board, and he ordered the pilot to take off and head for Mexico.

He also made a few strange demands: the cabin was not to be pressurized and the rear-exit ladder was to be lowered and locked open during takeoff. The pilot was to leave the landing gear down and to maintain a height of no more than ten thousand feet. What's more, the

113

flaps were to be set at fifteen degrees, which would produce an air speed of no more than 190 miles per hour.

Clearly, Cooper knew a great deal about the workings of the 727. He knew enough to feel confident that he could parachute from the plane. He strapped one of the parachutes to his back, tied the knapsack to his waist, and headed for the rear exit. Ten minutes after takeoff, as the plane approached a wilderness area crossed by the Columbia River, Cooper jumped into the dark night. The $200,000 was hanging from his waist.

A great manhunt was set up to find Cooper and the money. It was a strange robbery, and although it seemed well planned, there were some loopholes. First, Cooper had no idea of the pilot's flight plan that evening. He had no way of knowing where he would jump. Second, he seemed to have wanted to jump well before evening. Because of delays in landing and refueling at Seattle, Cooper jumped after nightfall. He didn't know where he was, and he was unable to see the obstacles that met him as he made his descent.

The FBI found no trace of Cooper or his stolen money. Nine years later, on February 10, 1980, the Ingram family was picnicking along the Columbia River. Eight-year-old Brian Ingram, preparing to build a fire, was smoothing the sand along the bank when he found three packets of money — $5,800 in all. Brian realized that the money must have been in the water for some time because its edges were worn off.

114

Wondering what Brian had found, the Ingrams took the money to FBI headquarters in Portland, where they discovered that the serial numbers on the bills matched those that had been given to Dan Cooper. Where was the other $194,200? And where was Dan Cooper?

Writer Richard Tosaw, who has researched the case thoroughly, believes that Cooper landed in the Columbia River that November night. Struggling to save himself, he probably cut the cords of the knapsack; disconnected, the bag would have sunk to the bottom of the riverbed, though perhaps a good way downstream. Then Cooper would have tried to free himself from the parachute. These would have been hard enough tasks in full daylight and warm water. But it was night and the Columbia River was icy. According to Tosaw, Cooper probably drowned that night. Eventually, the money bag would have rotted, freeing the money to flow with the river. Some washed up along the bank, but the rest of the money, Tosaw believes, is beneath the river. No one knows when more of it is likely to surface.

Treasure Hint
To uncover clues about Dan Cooper's loot, you need to pinpoint the area over which he jumped and the exact location where Brian Ingram found the money. You can do this by reading newspaper articles about the skyjacking and Brian Ingram's discovery. Then you and your family might make some camping trips to the area and begin hunting along the banks of the Columbia River.

Site Clue 5: Local legends

Most towns have tales of a missing treasure or two. As a treasure tracker, you may not have any idea whether such stories are true, but you may want to investigate them — just in case.

One local legend in Jackson, Tennessee, concerns the Woolfork family, according to researcher Howard M. Duffy. John Woolfork, who owned a plantation on Cotton Grove Road, died just before the start of the Civil War. His wife, who inherited the estate, kept her fortune at home. When the Civil War began, Union troops were on the march and Mrs. Woolfork was worried that the house might be ransacked and her money stolen. One night she took a sack of gold coins and by lantern light buried them in a shallow ditch along a line of cedars on the west side of the house.

Although the soldiers never came, Mrs. Woolfork left the coins buried. Not long afterward, she fell ill and, shortly before she died, pointed out their location to her nine-year-old daughter, Anna.

After the war, Anna and other members of her family tried to locate the cache of coins but failed. Many believe that the coins are still there. As Duffy writes, "When last heard of, the property was owned by Mrs. R. E. McLeary."

Is the legend based on fact? Does the treasure still exist? One day a dedicated treasure tracker in Madison County, Tennessee, will undoubtedly find out.

Treasure Hint

Once you come across a local legend, check the source. Try to find the date that the treasure was supposed to have been buried. Then search through the newspaper microfilms for that month or year to find clues about the legend.

Two treasure hunters followed much of the advice given in the last two chapters. They read a treasure-magazine story about a Belen, New Mexico, train robbery whose loot had never been found. On May 23, 1898, two robbers known as Bronco Bill and Kid Johnson jumped aboard the engine of a train as it stopped at the Belen depot. They forced the engineer at gunpoint to move the train a short way out of town, where they uncoupled the engine and the express car. They ordered the engineer to travel another half mile or so. Then they stopped the engine, gained access to the express car, and pushed an iron safe through the side door and onto the ground. They quickly blasted the safe open and stuffed their pockets with paper money and silver dollars. Afraid that a posse would come after them, the two robbers decided to bury their silver dollars between three trees on a small sand hill northwest of the tracks. They were eventually tracked down but killed two deputies in a shoot-out and escaped. A new posse cornered them two months later at the Double Circle Ranch in Arizona; this time Kid Johnson was killed and Bronco Bill was returned to New Mexico, where he spent twelve years in the Territorial Prison in Santa Fe before being paroled. According to the story, Bronco Bill tried to find the silver but soon gave up in frustration. He died a pauper.

The two men became so interested in the story that they decided to search for the missing money. Their first stop? Not the site of the robbery, but their library. They checked the references the author had consulted in writing his story. They located old stories in microfilmed Albuquerque newspapers which confirmed the account of the robbery. They also found the story mentioned in a regional treasure-hunting guide.

Convinced that the story was true and that the money remained hidden, they set out with their metal detectors for Belen. Their first find, in a sandy hill northwest of the railroad tracks, was an 1880 Morgan silver dollar that seemed to prove the train robbers had been in the area.

The two men dug deeper. A little over a foot down, they discovered a cache of 332 silver dollars. Most were in Extra Fine condition, a term coin collectors use to indicate that coins have not been put into wide circulation. Many of the silver dollars would now sell for forty dollars or more apiece.

Had they found the train-robbery cache? No train robber was about to ride up and ask for the money back. No one else could verify that these were the silver dollars taken from the train that day. But the two treasure hunters were certain they found the train-robbery loot. And they accomplished this, first and foremost, by researching the story.

1880 Morgan silver dollar

8. At the Treasure Site

When you get to a potential treasure site, remember that some treasure seekers have managed to give the hobby a bad name. Their greed and disregard for others as well as for the environment have endangered the future of the pastime. Consequently, a tracker must agree to abide by a number of rules in order not to cause further harm.

First, always ask for permission to hunt on private property.

Second, always fill holes that you dig, even if they are quite small. One hole may not damage an area, but a few holes can quickly pockmark an otherwise attractive landscape.

Third, don't litter. Be generous: even if you haven't left debris at the site, remove any trash you find.

Fourth, in well-populated areas restrict your treasure hunting to early morning or evening. If you choose to hunt for coins at high noon on a crowded beach, you'll only attract attention. It's better to get up early and search before anyone arrives.

Fifth, do not destroy anything historic. If you think you've discovered something of historical importance, such as an Indian village or a dinosaur burial ground, stop immediately and inform the proper authorities. An archaeologist will be better equipped to handle an excavation than you are.

Finally, never go treasure hunting alone. Trips to rural or wooded areas require a companion or two in case you encounter any problems. In fact, many people make treasure hunting a family hobby. Remember that a group of people can explore a potential treasure site in much less time. This may lead to greater rewards.

What are we looking for ??

At the site, two last tips may help you in your hunt.

Treasure Tip 1: Put yourself in the past

Many hunters think alike, and spots that once held treasure have been picked apart by greedy enthusiasts. Instead, think creatively and try to put yourself in the past. You must begin to think as if you were at the scene when the treasure was lost or hidden. By doing this, you can analyze the situation with a freshness that may lead you right to the valuables.

Take the case of the treasure still located on the south side of the Red River on the Texas-Oklahoma border. In 1892, Lewis Franklin Palmore was appointed the first federal marshal in Indian Territory, the area that is now Oklahoma. One of his first encounters with criminals occurred two years later. Four men robbed the First National Bank in Bowie, Texas, and headed north, stopping for the night on the south bank of the flooded Red River.

That night Palmore received a telegram from the city marshal of Bowie informing him that the robbers were headed for Indian Territory. Palmore realized that the robbers would have to ford the flooded river at Rock Crossing. The next morning, when the robbers saw that a posse was approaching from the south, they plunged into the river at Rock Crossing and swam beside their horses. Palmore and two deputies waited on the other

side and arrested them. In their saddlebags, Palmore found $18,000 in paper money, which had been divided evenly among them. Surprisingly, $10,000 in $20 gold pieces was nowhere to be found.

The robbers were taken to Fort Smith, Arkansas, where Judge Roy Parker conducted a trial and sentenced them to hang. With nooses around their necks, the robbers were seated on their horses, waiting for their execution. One of them leaned toward Palmore and told him that the gold coins had been hidden near the robbers' final campsite, on the south bank of the Red River. Although Palmore searched the area many times for the cache of coins, he never found it. He passed the story on to his son, Frank, who searched the site before metal detectors became popular.

Frank Palmore believes that to find the coins the treasure tracker must visualize the way the flooded river was in 1894. How high was the water? Where would the riverbanks have been? And where would the robbers have camped? Palmore says that a tracker might get help from local people who remember where Rock Crossing was. The coins will be found, Palmore writes, "somewhere between the bridge on Highway 81 and the mouth of the Little Wichita."

Treasure Tip 2: Be a good listener

If you see other people at the possible treasure site, you might want to ask them some questions about the area, without divulging your purpose.

One treasure hunter who listened well was New Yorker Michael Chaplan. His greatest desire was to find a cache, and so Chaplan decided to research the Lindbergh kidnapping of 1932, since all of the ransom money had not been recovered. What's more, the man convicted of the kidnapping had lived in one of New York's boroughs, so Chaplan thought it might be worth looking for the missing money.

After researching Bruno Richard Hauptmann, the convicted kidnapper, Chaplan discovered that each weekend Hauptmann had camped on Hunter Island, a 500-acre wilderness area — a perfect place to hide ransom

Yep, I remember exactly where he used to picnic! Seems like one time he had a shovel with him. I thought that was kinda funny so I followed him and watched him dig a hole, but then my mother called and I never did see what he buried there... or what he dug up!

money. On a trip to the island, Chaplan met a group of older picnickers. He questioned them about their knowledge of the island and learned that there was an old picnic area used by German and Slavic immigrants during the 1930s. Now it was forgotten; its wooden tables rotting and covered with vines.

Chaplan decided to search this area with his metal detector. His heart began to race when he heard a loud signal from his detector. Something was buried there — something large! He imagined a fortune, a treasure hunter's dream. What he found was a metal container and lots of . . . dishes: dinner and dessert plates, along with a soup tureen. Some picnickers had obviously decided to make their repeated trips easier and stored their dinnerware at the picnic grounds.

With hard work and perhaps some luck, the day will come when you, like Michael Chaplan, uncover your first treasure.

What should you do?

Bring a picnic lunch!

1. Fill out a treasure report.

Many treasure trackers keep a record of every discovery they make. In this way they can revisit the location to find more treasure. Sometimes it's not possible to explore a site thoroughly in one day; an accurate logbook will enable you to return.

Here's one version of a treasure log.

Treasure Log

DATE: _____
LOCATION: _____
_____
_____

TERRAIN: hills / mountains / embankment
(circle)   lake / pond / river / creek / stream
             woods / clearing / desert / plains
             valley / canyon / ditch

SOIL: sand / clay / mud / earth / other: _____
WEATHER: cloudy / sunny / rainy / snowy / ice
TREASURE SEARCHED: _____
TREASURE FOUND: _____
_____
_____

DIFFICULTIES ENCOUNTERED: _____
_____
_____
_____

MAP OF EXACT LOCATION:

2. Explore the history of what you've found.

To serious trackers, history is more than dates and facts learned in school. With every find, history becomes real and imaginable, something connected to their lives.

One young man, Benjamin Alfred Wetherill, grew interested in hunting treasure in 1881 when his family moved west to a ranch near Mancos, Colorado. He wanted to make his fortune and spent some time prospecting for gold. As he learned, though, gold hunting was a time-consuming process that rarely paid off. For a time, he was a rancher. Then he discovered something that changed his life and developed in him a profound respect for history.

In remote canyons around his ranch were many Indian ruins, cliff dwellings that were built and abandoned many years ago. Pottery fragments were everywhere. Wetherill and his brothers paid little attention to them, until the day he saw what he later called the Cliff Palace, a cliff dwelling so immense that it looked like a "small ruined city." He climbed a stone stairway and saw the remnants of an Indian civilization that had lived and

disappeared long ago. As he described it in his autobiography:

> Things were arranged in the rooms as if the people might just have been out visiting somewhere. Perfect specimens of pottery sat on the floors . . . ; household equipment [was] where the housewives had last used the articles; evidence of children playing house even as children do now. . . . There was no indication of violence toward the people themselves, but the greater part of the immense buildings had been pulled apart and the timbers in the roofs and floors removed.

He wanted to learn more about the inhabitants and tried to persuade the United States government to undertake an excavation of this ruin and others; the government was not interested. So Wetherill and his brothers attempted to study the cliff dwellings themselves. Even though they could not support their work financially, they arranged to hire workers to excavate the ruin. Unfortunately, they did not keep detailed records of the location of each treasure, which eventually led to the charge that Wetherill and his brothers were "pothunters," interested only in stealing pottery from the ruins and selling it for profit.

When in 1906 the government finally created the Mesa Verde National Park at the site, the Wetherills were blamed for the destruction of the ruins and the theft of its property.

Although Benjamin Wetherill was not a highly educated man, his experience in the ruins — during the years when archaeology was far from the science it's considered today — helped others understand the people who were the cliff dwellers. He not only developed his own appreciation of history but encouraged others to do the same.

3. Decide what you want to do with the treasure.

Finding something is one thing; deciding its fate is another. Ask yourself the following questions:

IS THE OWNER IDENTIFIABLE ?

Many people do not want to keep anything that belongs to someone else — even if it is worth a lot of money. They will track down the owner of an object, when there are clues to his or her identity. This is relatively easy to do when the treasure is a piece of jewelry such as a class ring.

One man who returned a class ring was Wayne Schutts. He found it along the sandy beach of Waikiki in 1985. He could tell that the ring wasn't particularly valuable. Rather than throwing it away or trying to sell it, Schutts inspected the ring, which bore the U.S. Naval Academy's name, the date 1934, and the initials R.O. A good researcher, Schutts contacted the Naval Academy and looked up the initials in the 1934 yearbook.

There he found the name Richard O'Kane, now a retired rear admiral.

The Naval Academy helped Schutts contact O'Kane, who was surprised that someone had found his class ring. After all, he had given it to his wife, Ernestine, who had lost it in 1937 as she swam at Waikiki Beach.

The return of an inexpensive class ring was a priceless experience for both the O'Kanes and Schutts.

SHOULD THE TREASURE BE SOLD?

This is an option most trackers don't choose. First, most treasures aren't valuable enough to sell. Second, even if your treasure is salable, you are required to pay a hefty tax on the profit. Finally, you have to find a buyer. Remember that the value of your treasure is enhanced by the thrill of finding it yourself. Selling a treasure isn't as much fun as finding one. Instead, you may want to start a collection of your treasures and display them at home.

IS THE TREASURE TOO VALUABLE OR IMPORTANT TO KEEP?

Some treasure finders have such an interest in preserving their discoveries that they turn them over to a public museum. This is especially true of people who find very valuable items.

132

For example, on August 25, 1990, Cecil Hodder found a large cache of jewelry and coins in a field near Snettisham, England. Fortunately, Hodder had received permission from the landowner to search the field with his metal detector. The find proved to be the most valuable cache of Celtic gold and silver discovered in England.

What did Hodder do with the treasure? Under English law, he was entitled to keep anything that was *accidentally* lost. However, if the treasure was hidden *purposefully* so that it could be retrieved later, it is given to the government, although the finder receives a monetary reward.

"I don't care about the reward," Hodder told reporters. "All I am interested in is history."

The treasure, which is valued somewhere between $10,000,000 and $40,000,000, is now on display at its new permanent home: the British Museum, in London.

9. Developing a Talent for Treasure

Are you ready to find treasure? Here are some exercises you can use to sharpen your tracking skills.

Practice 1: Hunting for household treasures

You might want to refine your treasure-tracking skills by starting at home. Ask your grandparents, neighbors, or friends if they'd mind a household treasure hunt.

Once someone agrees, here are the treasures you might uncover and their locations.

Coins and jewelry.

There are three places to check. First, inspect all furniture, especially upholstered chairs and couches. Not only should you remove the cushions, but you should wedge your hand between the bottom and the side of the chair. This is an excellent location for hidden coins.

Second, check the space between the floor and any wall moldings in older houses. Usually, if the room is uncarpeted, you can easily spot the joint where the wall meets the flooring; any number of coins could have fallen there. If the room is carpeted, ask for permission and get help before attempting to lift the carpeting; and watch for carpet tacks as you do.

Finally, if the doors in the house are equipped with mortise-type locks and have rather large keyholes, a child may have dropped coins or jewelry into the lock. Again, be sure to have help if you're going to remove a lock. If it's old, you may not be able to replace it.

Children's belongings.

Search the cellar, attic, closets, and garage for the following valuable items:

Baseball cards. Baseball cards have become real treasures, especially older ones in mint condition. Did an uncle or aunt, grandfather or grandmother, great-grandfather or great-grandmother, ever collect baseball cards as a child?

Marbles. Think twice before throwing away old marbles. According to treasure hunter Joe Clark, one man sold two hundred marbles he had found for about $175.

Teddy bears and other stuffed animals. A teddy bear can be worth a small fortune. In 1989, for example, one old bear sold for more than $22,000 in an auction in England.

Dolls and other toys. Dolls and toys have become valuable as well, even ones that are only a few years old. Their value depends on their quality, condition, and rarity. Even a Barbie doll can be worth money, especially if it is still packaged in its original box and has never been used.

Practice 2: Drawing a treasure map

As a treasure hunter, you will have to draw a map of the location of each discovery you make. If you find a coin in a farmer's field one day, you may want to return another day and look for more. The coin, after all, could be part of a cache.

To practice your map-making skills, use your school playground or your backyard. Follow these directions:

Put a coin or another small object somewhere on the site you've chosen. It should be hidden from sight, even if it is only placed in the grass.

Draw the site area on a sheet of paper. Make sure you indicate any important landmarks. For example, if

137

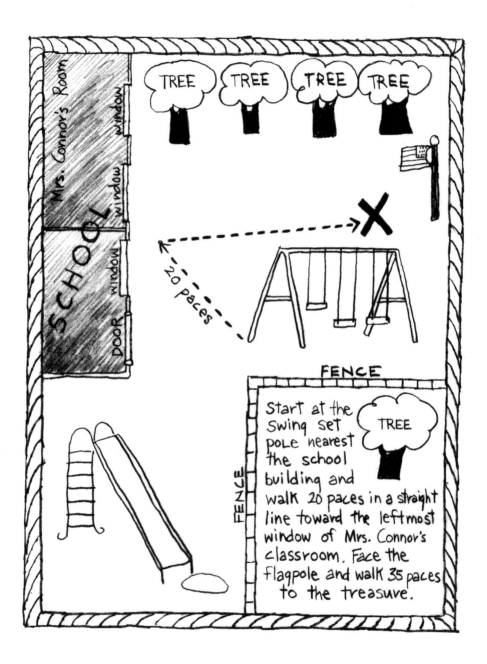

you're using a playground, show where the swings or other playground equipment is. Then mark the treasure with an **X**.

Indicate distances from the landmarks to the treasure.
Since you won't always have a tape measure, rely on your own two feet and count off paces. Place one foot carefully in front of the other and walk from each landmark to the treasure. Write the number of paces on the map.

Write directions for finding the treasure. You must be very specific in telling others where to start. For example, you cannot write: "Start at the swings and walk 20 paces north." The swing set may have six swings, so you'll need to direct the person to start from a specific place: "Start at the swing-set pole nearest the school building." What's more, telling the person to walk north is not specific enough. You might write: "Walk 20 paces in a straight line toward the leftmost window of Mrs. Connor's third-grade classroom." Altogether, then, your directions will be quite long: "Start at the swing-set pole nearest the school building and walk 20 paces in a staight line toward the leftmost window of Mrs. Connor's third-grade classroom." By making your directions clear and providing a map, you will help someone find the treasure you've hidden.

Give the map to friends or family members and ask them to find the treasure. If you've drawn a good map and written good directions, they should be able to locate the treasure. If not, go back to the drawing board and try again. Remember that success in finding the treasure depends on the accuracy of your paces — and the size of the other person's feet may be different from yours.

Practice 3: Cipher reading

If you're interested in solving the Beale ciphers or other treasure codes, you must practice your deciphering skills. A treasure tracker will learn complicated ciphers and practice them with friends or family. Here are two types of ciphers to learn.

Substitution cipher. The most common substitution cipher is the reverse-alphabet cipher: A = Z, B = Y, C = X, and so forth.

A B C D E F G H I J K L M N O P Q R S T U V W X Y Z
Z Y X W V U T S R Q P O N M L K J I H G F E D C B A

It doesn't take a genius to solve a code written in this cipher.

RHM'G GSRH GLL VZHB ?

A somewhat less common, but still easy, substitution cipher was preferred by Julius Caesar. Two Confederate generals, A. S. Johnson and Pierre Beauregard, used Caesar's cipher during the Battle of Shiloh.

Caesar's cipher (when translated into English) looks like this:

A B C D E F G H I J K L M N O P Q R S T U V W X Y Z
D E F G H I J K L M N O P Q R S T U V W X Y Z A B C

As you can see, Caesar merely substituted the letter that was three places away. You could easily create your own substitution cipher, using a variation of Caesar's method.

The problem with substitution ciphers, however, is that they are too easy to break. Remember that the reason for using code is to keep your message safe, perhaps out of enemy hands. By making a simple substitution, the decoder has not changed the frequency with which a letter will appear; this will help a decoding expert break the code.

Here's why: the most frequently used English letter is *E*; about one eighth of any text consists of the letter *E*. A decoding expert will be on the lookout for the most frequent letters; after *E*, they are *T, A, O, N, I, R, S,* and *H*. Once the expert has placed these letters, the message should be 70 percent solved.

⊥H∩R∩ ∩R∩ V∩RY MANY ∩'S IN ∩NGLISH S∩N⊥∩NC∩S!

Mary Queen of Scots lost her head because a coded letter she had written (in which she planned the assassination of Queen Elizabeth I) was broken by Sir Francis Walsingham, who founded the British Secret Service. Her code was a substitution cipher that used symbols Mary had created. Although Mary was clever enough to pepper her coded letters with "nulls" (that is, symbols that had no meaning at all), her code was broken by determining letter frequency.

Key-word cipher. Obviously, anyone with an important message will want a cipher that cannot be broken by letter frequency. The key-word cipher, developed in the fifteenth century by Italian architect Leon Alberti, fits the bill. Alberti's cipher uses the following table:

Key-Word Letters

	A	B	C	D	E	F	G	H	I	J	K	L	M	N	O	P	Q	R	S	T	U	V	W	X	Y	Z
A	a	b	c	d	e	f	g	h	i	j	k	l	m	n	o	p	q	r	s	t	u	v	w	x	y	z
B	b	c	d	e	f	g	h	i	j	k	l	m	n	o	p	q	r	s	t	u	v	w	x	y	z	a
C	c	d	e	f	g	h	i	j	k	l	m	n	o	p	q	r	s	t	u	v	w	x	y	z	a	b
D	d	e	f	g	h	i	j	k	l	m	n	o	p	q	r	s	t	u	v	w	x	y	z	a	b	c
E	e	f	g	h	i	j	k	l	m	n	o	p	q	r	s	t	u	v	w	x	y	z	a	b	c	d
F	f	g	h	i	j	k	l	m	n	o	p	q	r	s	t	u	v	w	x	y	z	a	b	c	d	e
G	g	h	i	j	k	l	m	n	o	p	q	r	s	t	u	v	w	x	y	z	a	b	c	d	e	f
H	h	i	j	k	l	m	n	o	p	q	r	s	t	u	v	w	x	y	z	a	b	c	d	e	f	g
I	i	j	k	l	m	n	o	p	q	r	s	t	u	v	w	x	y	z	a	b	c	d	e	f	g	h
J	j	k	l	m	n	o	p	q	r	s	t	u	v	w	x	y	z	a	b	c	d	e	f	g	h	i
K	k	l	m	n	o	p	q	r	s	t	u	v	w	x	y	z	a	b	c	d	e	f	g	h	i	j
L	l	m	n	o	p	q	r	s	t	u	v	w	x	y	z	a	b	c	d	e	f	g	h	i	j	k
M	m	n	o	p	q	r	s	t	u	v	w	x	y	z	a	b	c	d	e	f	g	h	i	j	k	l
N	n	o	p	q	r	s	t	u	v	w	x	y	z	a	b	c	d	e	f	g	h	i	j	k	l	m
O	o	p	q	r	s	t	u	v	w	x	y	z	a	b	c	d	e	f	g	h	i	j	k	l	m	n
P	p	q	r	s	t	u	v	w	x	y	z	a	b	c	d	e	f	g	h	i	j	k	l	m	n	o
Q	q	r	s	t	u	v	w	x	y	z	a	b	c	d	e	f	g	h	i	j	k	l	m	n	o	p
R	r	s	t	u	v	w	x	y	z	a	b	c	d	e	f	g	h	i	j	k	l	m	n	o	p	q
S	s	t	u	v	w	x	y	z	a	b	c	d	e	f	g	h	i	j	k	l	m	n	o	p	q	r
T	t	u	v	w	x	y	z	a	b	c	d	e	f	g	h	i	j	k	l	m	n	o	p	q	r	s
U	u	v	w	x	y	z	a	b	c	d	e	f	g	h	i	j	k	l	m	n	o	p	q	r	s	t
V	v	w	x	y	z	a	b	c	d	e	f	g	h	i	j	k	l	m	n	o	p	q	r	s	t	u
W	w	x	y	z	a	b	c	d	e	f	g	h	i	j	k	l	m	n	o	p	q	r	s	t	u	v
X	x	y	z	a	b	c	d	e	f	g	h	i	j	k	l	m	n	o	p	q	r	s	t	u	v	w
Y	y	z	a	b	c	d	e	f	g	h	i	j	k	l	m	n	o	p	q	r	s	t	u	v	w	x
Z	z	a	b	c	d	e	f	g	h	i	j	k	l	m	n	o	p	q	r	s	t	u	v	w	x	y

To use the table, you will need a message and a key word. Let's say your message is LOOK UNDER THE STONE BY THE CELLAR DOOR. To send the message, you will need a key word (or a password) to encode the message. The word can be whatever you choose, although it should not repeat any letter. In this case, we'll use the key word EARLY.

To encode the message, first write your message without spaces. Second, write the key word repeatedly above the message, until you come to the end of the message, as shown below:

Third, locate the first letter of the key word (*E*) across the top of the table *and* the first letter of the message (*L*) along the left-hand side of the table. Draw (or imagine) lines from each letter until they intersect. The letter you find at the intersection becomes the first letter of the code.

Here's an example, using the first word of the message: LOOK.

Key-Word Letters

	A	B	C	D	E	F	G	H	I	J	K	L	M	N	O	P	Q	R	S	T	U	V	W	X	Y	Z
A	a	b	c	d	e	f	g	h	i	j	k	l	m	n	o	p	q	r	s	t	u	v	w	x	y	z
B	b	c	d	e	f	g	h	i	j	k	l	m	n	o	p	q	r	s	t	u	v	w	x	y	z	a
C	c	d	e	f	g	h	i	j	k	l	m	n	o	p	q	r	s	t	u	v	w	x	y	z	a	b
D	d	e	f	g	h	i	j	k	l	m	n	o	p	q	r	s	t	u	v	w	x	y	z	a	b	c
E	e	f	g	h	i	j	k	l	m	n	o	p	q	r	s	t	u	v	w	x	y	z	a	b	c	d
F	f	g	h	i	j	k	l	m	n	o	p	q	r	s	t	u	v	w	x	y	z	a	b	c	d	e
G	g	h	i	j	k	l	m	n	o	p	q	r	s	t	u	v	w	x	y	z	a	b	c	d	e	f
H	h	i	j	k	l	m	n	o	p	q	r	s	t	u	v	w	x	y	z	a	b	c	d	e	f	g
I	i	j	k	l	m	n	o	p	q	r	s	t	u	v	w	x	y	z	a	b	c	d	e	f	g	h
J	j	k	l	m	n	o	p	q	r	s	t	u	v	w	x	y	z	a	b	c	d	e	f	g	h	i
K	k	l	m	n	o	p	q	r	s	t	u	v	w	x	y	z	a	b	c	d	e	f	g	h	i	j
L	l	m	n	o	ⓟ	q	r	s	t	u	v	w	x	y	z	a	b	c	d	e	f	g	h	i	j	k
M	m	n	o	p	q	r	s	t	u	v	w	x	y	z	a	b	c	d	e	f	g	h	i	j	k	l
N	n	o	p	q	r	s	t	u	v	w	x	y	z	a	b	c	d	e	f	g	h	i	j	k	l	m
O	o	p	q	r	s	t	u	v	w	x	y	z	a	b	c	d	e	f	g	h	i	j	k	l	m	n
P	p	q	r	s	t	u	v	w	x	y	z	a	b	c	d	e	f	g	h	i	j	k	l	m	n	o
Q	q	r	s	t	u	v	w	x	y	z	a	b	c	d	e	f	g	h	i	j	k	l	m	n	o	p
R	r	s	t	u	v	w	x	y	z	a	b	c	d	e	f	g	h	i	j	k	l	m	n	o	p	q
S	s	t	u	v	w	x	y	z	a	b	c	d	e	f	g	h	i	j	k	l	m	n	o	p	q	r
T	t	u	v	w	x	y	z	a	b	c	d	e	f	g	h	i	j	k	l	m	n	o	p	q	r	s
U	u	v	w	x	y	z	a	b	c	d	e	f	g	h	i	j	k	l	m	n	o	p	q	r	s	t
V	v	w	x	y	z	a	b	c	d	e	f	g	h	i	j	k	l	m	n	o	p	q	r	s	t	u
W	w	x	y	z	a	b	c	d	e	f	g	h	i	j	k	l	m	n	o	p	q	r	s	t	u	v
X	x	y	z	a	b	c	d	e	f	g	h	i	j	k	l	m	n	o	p	q	r	s	t	u	v	w
Y	y	z	a	b	c	d	e	f	g	h	i	j	k	l	m	n	o	p	q	r	s	t	u	v	w	x
Z	z	a	b	c	d	e	f	g	h	i	j	k	l	m	n	o	p	q	r	s	t	u	v	w	x	y

Key-Word Letters

	A	B	C	D	E	F	G	H	I	J	K	L	M	N	O	P	Q	R	S	T	U	V	W	X	Y	Z
A	a	b	c	d	e	f	g	h	i	j	k	l	m	n	o	p	q	r	s	t	u	v	w	x	y	z
B	b	c	d	e	f	g	h	i	j	k	l	m	n	o	p	q	r	s	t	u	v	w	x	y	z	a
C	c	d	e	f	g	h	i	j	k	l	m	n	o	p	q	r	s	t	u	v	w	x	y	z	a	b
D	d	e	f	g	h	i	j	k	l	m	n	o	p	q	r	s	t	u	v	w	x	y	z	a	b	c
E	e	f	g	h	i	j	k	l	m	n	o	p	q	r	s	t	u	v	w	x	y	z	a	b	c	d
F	f	g	h	i	j	k	l	m	n	o	p	q	r	s	t	u	v	w	x	y	z	a	b	c	d	e
G	g	h	i	j	k	l	m	n	o	p	q	r	s	t	u	v	w	x	y	z	a	b	c	d	e	f
H	h	i	j	k	l	m	n	o	p	q	r	s	t	u	v	w	x	y	z	a	b	c	d	e	f	g
I	i	j	k	l	m	n	o	p	q	r	s	t	u	v	w	x	y	z	a	b	c	d	e	f	g	h
J	j	k	l	m	n	o	p	q	r	s	t	u	v	w	x	y	z	a	b	c	d	e	f	g	h	i
K	k	l	m	n	o	p	q	r	s	t	u	v	w	x	y	z	a	b	c	d	e	f	g	h	i	j
L	l	m	n	o	p	q	r	s	t	u	v	w	x	y	z	a	b	c	d	e	f	g	h	i	j	k
M	m	n	o	p	q	r	s	t	u	v	w	x	y	z	a	b	c	d	e	f	g	h	i	j	k	l
N	n	o	p	q	r	s	t	u	v	w	x	y	z	a	b	c	d	e	f	g	h	i	j	k	l	m
O	⊚	p	q	r	s	t	u	v	w	x	y	z	a	b	c	d	e	f	g	h	i	j	k	l	m	n
P	p	q	r	s	t	u	v	w	x	y	z	a	b	c	d	e	f	g	h	i	j	k	l	m	n	o
Q	q	r	s	t	u	v	w	x	y	z	a	b	c	d	e	f	g	h	i	j	k	l	m	n	o	p
R	r	s	t	u	v	w	x	y	z	a	b	c	d	e	f	g	h	i	j	k	l	m	n	o	p	q
S	s	t	u	v	w	x	y	z	a	b	c	d	e	f	g	h	i	j	k	l	m	n	o	p	q	r
T	t	u	v	w	x	y	z	a	b	c	d	e	f	g	h	i	j	k	l	m	n	o	p	q	r	s
U	u	v	w	x	y	z	a	b	c	d	e	f	g	h	i	j	k	l	m	n	o	p	q	r	s	t
V	v	w	x	y	z	a	b	c	d	e	f	g	h	i	j	k	l	m	n	o	p	q	r	s	t	u
W	w	x	y	z	a	b	c	d	e	f	g	h	i	j	k	l	m	n	o	p	q	r	s	t	u	v
X	x	y	z	a	b	c	d	e	f	g	h	i	j	k	l	m	n	o	p	q	r	s	t	u	v	w
Y	y	z	a	b	c	d	e	f	g	h	i	j	k	l	m	n	o	p	q	r	s	t	u	v	w	x
Z	z	a	b	c	d	e	f	g	h	i	j	k	l	m	n	o	p	q	r	s	t	u	v	w	x	y

Key-Word Letters

	A	B	C	D	E	F	G	H	I	J	K	L	M	N	O	P	Q	R	S	T	U	V	W	X	Y	Z
A	a	b	c	d	e	f	g	h	i	j	k	l	m	n	o	p	q	r	s	t	u	v	w	x	y	z
B	b	c	d	e	f	g	h	i	j	k	l	m	n	o	p	q	r	s	t	u	v	w	x	y	z	a
C	c	d	e	f	g	h	i	j	k	l	m	n	o	p	q	r	s	t	u	v	w	x	y	z	a	b
D	d	e	f	g	h	i	j	k	l	m	n	o	p	q	r	s	t	u	v	w	x	y	z	a	b	c
E	e	f	g	h	i	j	k	l	m	n	o	p	q	r	s	t	u	v	w	x	y	z	a	b	c	d
F	f	g	h	i	j	k	l	m	n	o	p	q	r	s	t	u	v	w	x	y	z	a	b	c	d	e
G	g	h	i	j	k	l	m	n	o	p	q	r	s	t	u	v	w	x	y	z	a	b	c	d	e	f
H	h	i	j	k	l	m	n	o	p	q	r	s	t	u	v	w	x	y	z	a	b	c	d	e	f	g
I	i	j	k	l	m	n	o	p	q	r	s	t	u	v	w	x	y	z	a	b	c	d	e	f	g	h
J	j	k	l	m	n	o	p	q	r	s	t	u	v	w	x	y	z	a	b	c	d	e	f	g	h	i
K	k	l	m	n	o	p	q	r	s	t	u	v	w	x	y	z	a	b	c	d	e	f	g	h	i	j
L	l	m	n	o	p	q	r	s	t	u	v	w	x	y	z	a	b	c	d	e	f	g	h	i	j	k
M	m	n	o	p	q	r	s	t	u	v	w	x	y	z	a	b	c	d	e	f	g	h	i	j	k	l
N	n	o	p	q	r	s	t	u	v	w	x	y	z	a	b	c	d	e	f	g	h	i	j	k	l	m
O	o	p	q	r	s	t	u	v	w	x	y	z	a	b	c	d	e	f	g	h	i	j	k	l	m	n
P	p	q	r	s	t	u	v	w	x	y	z	a	b	c	d	e	f	g	h	i	j	k	l	m	n	o
Q	q	r	s	t	u	v	w	x	y	z	a	b	c	d	e	f	g	h	i	j	k	l	m	n	o	p
R	r	s	t	u	v	w	x	y	z	a	b	c	d	e	f	g	h	i	j	k	l	m	n	o	p	q
S	s	t	u	v	w	x	y	z	a	b	c	d	e	f	g	h	i	j	k	l	m	n	o	p	q	r
T	t	u	v	w	x	y	z	a	b	c	d	e	f	g	h	i	j	k	l	m	n	o	p	q	r	s
U	u	v	w	x	y	z	a	b	c	d	e	f	g	h	i	j	k	l	m	n	o	p	q	r	s	t
V	v	w	x	y	z	a	b	c	d	e	f	g	h	i	j	k	l	m	n	o	p	q	r	s	t	u
W	w	x	y	z	a	b	c	d	e	f	g	h	i	j	k	l	m	n	o	p	q	r	s	t	u	v
X	x	y	z	a	b	c	d	e	f	g	h	i	j	k	l	m	n	o	p	q	r	s	t	u	v	w
Y	y	z	a	b	c	d	e	f	g	h	i	j	k	l	m	n	o	p	q	r	s	t	u	v	w	x
Z	z	a	b	c	d	e	f	g	h	i	j	k	l	m	n	o	p	q	r	s	t	u	v	w	x	y

Key-Word Letters

A B C D E F G H I J K L M N O P Q R S T U V W X Y Z

A a b c d e f g h i j k l m n o p q r s t u v w x y z
B b c d e f g h i j k l m n o p q r s t u v w x y z a
C c d e f g h i j k l m n o p q r s t u v w x y z a b
D d e f g h i j k l m n o p q r s t u v w x y z a b c
E e f g h i j k l m n o p q r s t u v w x y z a b c d
F f g h i j k l m n o p q r s t u v w x y z a b c d e
G g h i j k l m n o p q r s t u v w x y z a b c d e f
H h i j k l m n o p q r s t u v w x y z a b c d e f g
I i j k l m n o p q r s t u v w x y z a b c d e f g h
J j k l m n o p q r s t u v w x y z a b c d e f g h i
K k l m n o p q r s t u (v) w x y z a b c d e f g h i j
L l m n o p q r s t u v w x y z a b c d e f g h i j k
M m n o p q r s t u v w x y z a b c d e f g h i j k l
N n o p q r s t u v w x y z a b c d e f g h i j k l m
O o p q r s t u v w x y z a b c d e f g h i j k l m n
P p q r s t u v w x y z a b c d e f g h i j k l m n o
Q q r s t u v w x y z a b c d e f g h i j k l m n o p
R r s t u v w x y z a b c d e f g h i j k l m n o p q
S s t u v w x y z a b c d e f g h i j k l m n o p q r
T t u v w x y z a b c d e f g h i j k l m n o p q r s
U u v w x y z a b c d e f g h i j k l m n o p q r s t
V v w x y z a b c d e f g h i j k l m n o p q r s t u
W w x y z a b c d e f g h i j k l m n o p q r s t u v
X x y z a b c d e f g h i j k l m n o p q r s t u v w
Y y z a b c d e f g h i j k l m n o p q r s t u v w x
Z z a b c d e f g h i j k l m n o p q r s t u v w x y

POFV = LOOK!

The code for LOOK will be:

> P (intersection of E and L),
> O (intersection of A and O),
> F (intersection of R and O), and
> V (intersection of L and K).

Try to encode the rest of the message; it is given (upside-down) at the bottom of this page.

As you encoded the message, did you notice that a repeated letter usually received a different code letter each time — as long as a different key-word letter appeared above the repeated letter? Did you notice, too, that the only repeated code letters were RLE (for THE)? Because this appeared twice (and because *the* is the most frequently used English word), a code breaker would be able to solve the code in no time. In this case, a longer key word might have helped. It would also have helped to break the code into units of equal length, so as not to indicate the length of the words. For example, rather than sending a message as MEET AT THE PARK

The code is POFV SRDC CRLE JEMQ ESJR LETP JPAI OMSR.

149

AFTER SCHOOL, you would write it (before encoding) as follows:

MEE TAT THE PAR KAF TER SCH OOL.

Once you encode the message, a code breaker won't know how long any of the words are. This will slow down his or her work.

A final note: if you're going to send a message written in a key-word cipher to a friend, you must also provide the key word (or clues that will help determine it). Without that word, your friend will have nothing but TROUBLE!

VFBA SLXN CONJ ZRLG ITAW ILFZ
PFCC HLOL CHIE CCHZ ZYKN OSUZ
FXTC GJYK TKFY BDYK VHLB NOXI

Practice 4: Burying your own treasure

One project you may want to undertake is the creation of your own treasure. For this, you and your family or your friends can assemble items that may have value or special meaning.

Author Alistair Reid, his twelve-year-old son, Jasper,

and a friend, Jeff Lerner, decided to bury their own treasure while on vacation in St. Andrews, Scotland. During the spring of 1971, they took a plastic box and filled it with treasure:

a history exam

three small plastic airplanes

a jarful of pennies

photographs of the family

a piece of white quartz

a pen that still wrote

a postcard of St. Andrews

a local newspaper dated May 22, 1971

TREASURE

Carrying spades and lanterns at twilight, they found the perfect burial spot on public land that bordered a local golf course. They selected a small elm tree, about twenty yards from a stone wall, as a landmark, then Jasper measured the distance from the tree to the treasure site: three arm spans. They told themselves they would remember the exact location when they returned to reclaim the box on Jasper's twenty-first birthday: August 9, 1980.

On the precise date nine years later, Reid, Jasper, and Jeff met in St. Andrews. The small elm tree was now fully grown — and problems developed with their memories. Jasper did not remember using "three arm spans" and began to pace off the distance from the tree. He dug a small hole at a location he chose and uncovered an unbroken teacup and a bent spoon — hardly his box of treasure. Even when he tried to measure by arm spans, he realized that his arm had been quite a bit shorter in 1971; precise measuring was impossible. By the time they found the box — with the aid of a metal detector — they had dug many holes in an area more than eighteen feet wide. Clearly, their memories of the twilight burial had dimmed in nine years.

Upon opening the box, they saw the announcement they had placed on top of their treasures. It read:

This chest, containing treasure in coin and various souvenirs of the present moment in St. Andrews in May, 1971, is buried here by Jasper Reid, Jeff Lerner, and Alistair Reid, in a spot known to these three persons. It is their intention to return on the 9th day of August, 1980, to meet and disinter the chest in one another's company and to celebrate their survival with appropriate ceremony. Sunday, May thirtieth, 1971, a hazy day with sea mist, rooks, curry, and kites.

To bury your own treasure, select a good box. It shouldn't be made of cardboard or even wood, which may rot over the years. A metal or plastic box with a tight seal is preferable. You may want to wrap the box in aluminum foil, since that will make retrieval with a metal detector easier.

152

Once you have your box, you can decide what you'd like to place in it. Different items may suit your purpose.

First, place some items that date the time you buried your treasure. For example, a copy of a recent newspaper is useful. This not only provides a date, but will be of interest in the future to see what was happening in your area and the world at the time.

Second, include a personal message. This could be written on paper or recorded on audio- or videotape. You may also want to encode a message so that its contents will remain secret until you decipher it. Your message might say who you are, what you've buried, why you've buried it, and what you hope to be doing in the future when you recover the box.

Third, include items that have personal meaning. Such items might include your favorite stuffed animal, a bedtime book you enjoy, or special toys that you've collected.

Finally, add possible future treasures. These could be shiny new coins, postage stamps, unopened packs of baseball cards, or whatever.

When you've assembled your collection, place it inside your box, perhaps wrapping everything in a plastic garbage bag or two in case it should spring a leak.

Then select a burial spot with care. First, avoid a place where you can be watched by others. As soon as you leave, someone may simply dig your box up. Second, bury it either on public land (where digging is allowed) or on your own property. If you decide to bury it in your backyard, consider whether your family is planning to move. If so, someone else will own your house and may not appreciate your digging there years from now.

When you've chosen a site, dig a hole at least two or three feet deep. If you bury your box too close to the surface, it may be uncovered by heavy rains or soil erosion. Finally, remind yourself when you wish to unearth your treasure. You might write a brief note, put it in an envelope, and ask your parents to place it in a safe-deposit box. The outside of the envelope might read: DO NOT OPEN UNTIL MAY 8, 2015 (or whatever date you choose). Inside, your note will describe the treasure you buried, along with a map of the location or written directions to the treasure. Whatever you do, however, do not rely on your memory of the burial. As you saw with Alistair and Jasper Reid, memory is a very tricky thing.

Practice 5: Start a treasure-finding service

You can get lots of hunting practice by beginning a finder's service. A metal detector will come in handy, but you can do visual searching, too. After all, your best resource is probably your brain and its ability to answer the question: *where can that treasure be?*

Make a card or poster that announces your service.

154

When someone calls you, always volunteer to find lost treasure *for free*. This may have its own rewards. One woman told Ohio treasure finder Richard Martin: "I'd sure like you to find a diamond ring my mother lost back here in 1950. Anything else you find is yours, and this yard has been a gathering place for kids a long time." With his metal detector, Martin not only found the ring, but also uncovered five silver coins and a small opal ring that the owner of the house didn't recognize.

You can also help when tragedy strikes. If a neighbor's house burns down, you can offer to help locate any valuables in the rubble. Treasure finder James Bruner did just that when a house in his Virginia neighborhood burned. The owners had tried to find a set of wedding rings and failed. There was too much burned metal in the ashes to use the detector, so Bruner sifted through the ashes by hand. He found the three rings, and also "a half gallon of coins." What's more, the owners themselves had come within two feet of finding the rings, but had become frustrated.

Now that you've perfected your tracking skills, you may be ready to investigate a few more tales about treasure.

10. Two Lost Treasures?

Although treasure stories may lead to the same conclusion — that gold or silver is buried somewhere — they may have different versions, and a treasure seeker can become quite perplexed. Such is the case with a treasure associated with the death of General George Armstrong Custer.

For many Americans living in 1876, the western part of the United States held the promise of great riches. Gold had been discovered in California, and in the early 1870s many were certain that huge amounts of the ore would be found in Montana and the Black Hills of South Dakota. Some small gold claims had already been filed there, but few struck it rich.

What the miners didn't know is that a lost shipment of gold was — and may still be — buried near the Little Bighorn battle site. When Custer and his men died in the valley of the Little Bighorn River on June 25, 1876, a steamboat named the *Far West* was making its way up the Bighorn River. Under the command of Captain Grant Marsh, the *Far West* had orders to follow the Bighorn River to the mouth of the Little Bighorn. Captain Marsh was then to guide the boat fifteen to twenty miles upstream and rendezvous with General Alfred H. Terry and resupply his troops. As the boat sailed to its destination, word reached Captain Marsh that Custer and his men had been massacred and that wounded soldiers would be brought to the *Far West* and taken to Fort Lincoln, near Bismarck, North Dakota.

The story of the *Far West* becomes confusing at this point. Some researchers agree that gold was on board the supply boat, but they disagree on how it got there. What's more, they agree that the gold was buried on-shore, but they disagree on its precise location. In fact, two stories have been told to account for the appearance — and disappearance — of the *Far West* gold.

Treasure Tale 1: Gold bars from Williston

According to an account by writer Emile Schurmacher, Captain Marsh had taken the boat to Williston, North Dakota, where it had collected a shipment of gold bars worth $375,000 and then left for its rendezvous with General Terry. The gold was to be delivered to Bismarck on the return trip.

After fifty-two wounded men were brought on board to make the 740-mile trip to Bismarck, Marsh realized that he would need all the room he had on board for firewood to fuel the steamer's engine. The gold would have to be buried ashore temporarily; he could return later to collect it.

Schurmacher says that Marsh twice attempted to retrieve the gold. Once, two months after it was hidden, he docked the boat in the same location. He could identify the site because tree stumps indicated where the crew had cut firewood to make the return journey to Bismarck. Unfortunately, heavy rains had caused a mud slide to wash over the burial site. Despite considerable digging, he and his men were unable to find even one bar of gold.

Treasure Tale 2: Gold nuggets from Bozeman

The other account, by writer Roy Norvill, is more dramatic. In it, Captain Marsh encountered three men on

159

the evening of June 26, the day after Custer's death. Marsh had not yet learned of the massacre, but he knew that many Sioux were in the area. The men shouted to Marsh from the riverbank. They were Gil Longworth, a wagon driver, and Tom Dickson and Mark Jergens, his guards. They were carrying a shipment of gold nuggets from Bozeman, Montana, to Bismarck. Longworth was worried that he would be attacked by the Sioux and would never deliver the gold shipment, so he begged Marsh to take it on board the *Far West*.

After it was transferred to the ship, Longworth, Dickson, and Jergens headed back to Bozeman on land, a route they considered safer. But Captain Marsh had second thoughts about keeping the gold on board. As he watched the smoke from many Sioux campsites that night, he concluded that it would be safer to hide the gold ashore and return for it later. This was accomplished the same night.

In the next few days, the wounded soldiers were brought to the steamer and Marsh learned the fate of the three men from Bozeman: All three were killed by the Sioux. Dickson and Jergens died at Pryor's Creek; Longworth's body was found a few days later at a spot known as Clark's Fork. Apparently, he had escaped the Sioux but had been mortally wounded in the process.

Norvill writes that although Marsh never forgot about the gold, he made no attempt to recover it. He was afraid that a return trip would be too risky. In 1879, however, he visited Bozeman to find the freight company that had hired Longworth. Unfortunately, the company had long since closed.

Two stories — and two versions of how the gold came to be on board the *Far West* and where it was buried.

Is either story true? Did Marsh load a shipment of gold bars in Williston, or did he accept a frightened driver's load of gold nuggets from Bozeman? Did he bury it on the Bighorn River, as Schurmacher claims, one-half mile from the Yellowstone River? Or did he bury it, as Norvill says, fifteen to twenty miles up the Bighorn River from the mouth of the Little Bighorn? Could there be two gold treasures? Or did one or both writers concoct intriguing stories?

Two things can be said for certain. First, Captain Grant Marsh and the *Far West* were real. Second, both helped in the evacuation of wounded soldiers and sailed the Bighorn and Little Bighorn rivers at the time of Custer's death.

Beyond that, however, nothing is clear. Although many people believe that a cache of gold is buried along the Bighorn River, a treasure tracker interested in this case should do a lot of library research before making a trip to the Bighorn River.

11. On the Treasure Trail

One late spring day in 1795, a sixteen-year-old farm boy named Daniel McGinnis left his home near Mahone Bay in Nova Scotia, Canada, and paddled his canoe to Oak Island, which was only two hundred yards offshore. Over the years, strange lights had been spotted there, and Daniel's neighbors had related interesting theories about the lights. Some thought that ghosts or other supernatural creatures inhabited the deserted island. Others believed that the infamous pirate Captain William Kidd had used the island as a base and had buried his treasure there. According to one local legend, two fishermen had rowed out to the island to investigate the nocturnal lights and had never been seen again.

Whether Daniel McGinnis believed in ghosts isn't recorded. What he did believe in, though, was the idea that Captain Kidd had buried treasure on the island.

163

Daniel also believed that he could locate the treasure. After all, the island was small — a mile long, a half mile wide — and would be easy to search.

As he crossed the heavily wooded island that day, he came to a clearing filled with tree stumps. These stumps indicated that someone had been on the island before. Could Captain Kidd's band of pirates have cleared the trees? This thought probably inspired Daniel to search the clearing carefully. He didn't stop to consider that the trees might have been cleared years earlier by the local Micmac tribe or by a lumberjack.

As Daniel scouted the clearing, he noticed a large oak tree standing in the center. A sturdy branch, perhaps fifteen feet from the ground, had been shortened to a length of four feet. Directly beneath this trimmed branch was a large circular indentation in the ground. It looked as if a large hole had been dug and then filled in, causing the earth to settle.

Daniel McGinnis was immediately convinced that he had found Captain Kidd's cache of treasure buried beside that oak tree. He realized that he would need tools and some help to find it. That night, he told two friends, sixteen-year-old Anthony Vaughan and twenty-one-year-old John Smith, about his discovery. They, too, were excited by the thought of finding a fortune buried under an oak tree.

The next day, the three young men, carrying shovels and picks, landed on the island and headed for the clearing, where they began to shovel earth from the center of the indentation. Two feet down, they hit what they said was a layer of flagstone; someone had obviously laid it there. As they cleared away the stones, they concluded that they were standing on a circular pit — now refilled with earth — perhaps thirteen feet in diameter. They wondered only briefly what the shaft contained. For, shortly after, they referred to it as the Money Pit.

Every day for a few weeks, the young men returned to the island to dig. By the time they had dug to a depth of thirty feet, they realized that recovering the treasure was going to take much more work. They encouraged their family, friends, and neighbors to join them in the dig, but no one was interested. After all, Mahone Bay was inhabited by hardworking farmers and fishermen who could not take the time for boyish adventure. So the same summer Smith and McGinnis bought land on the island and moved there, while Vaughan stayed close by on the mainland, since his family owned most of the land that bordered the coast across from the island. Then the three men tried to find investors who would support their treasure search.

By the time they succeeded, it was 1803. That summer, workers dug to a depth of ninety feet, uncovering something later identified as coconut fiber, even though the nearest coconut trees were more than fifteen hundred miles away. They also found a stone supposedly inscribed with a strange code. As they removed it, they noticed that the earth in the shaft was becoming so muddy that they had to bail out two buckets of water for every bucket of dirt.

One day, just before nightfall, at a depth of ninety-eight feet, the workers struck a hard object in the mud. Since some of the workers thought it was wooden, many concluded that it was a chest. They stopped for the day, anticipating a fast and rewarding conclusion to the mys-

166

tery of the Money Pit. The next morning, however, they found that the shaft was filled with sixty feet of seawater. No matter how hard they tried to bail the water, they could not lower the water level.

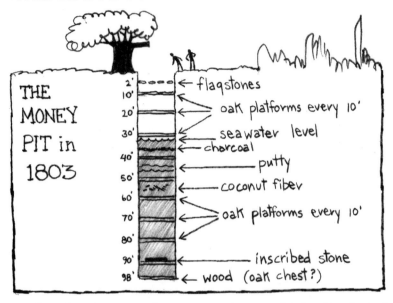

THE MONEY PIT in 1803

2' 10' 20' 30' 40' 50' 60' 70' 80' 90' 98'

← flagstones
← oak platforms every 10'
← seawater level
← charcoal
← putty
← coconut fiber
← oak platforms every 10'
← inscribed stone
← wood (oak chest?)

By the time another excavation could be funded, it was 1849. Daniel McGinnis was dead, but Anthony Vaughan and John Smith were still hopeful that the treasure would be found. In the excavation of 1849, evidence of a structure more than ninety-eight feet below the surface was uncovered. Since the workers had never been able to drain the flooded shaft, a drill bit with a hollow center was used to gather a sample of whatever material the drill encountered. This structure appeared

167

to have a 6-inch layer of spruce, 4 inches of oak, 22 inches of metal in pieces, 8 inches of oak, 22 more inches of metal, 4 inches of oak, and 6 inches of spruce. The apparent symmetry of this finding was interpreted to mean that two oaken treasure chests, partitioned by spruce platforms, were stacked upon each other. Unfortunately, the drill was unable to retrieve any of the metal pieces that filled the two 22-inch spaces.

But the excavation team did manage to provide evidence that the Money Pit was man made — and booby-trapped. At low tide a small stream trickled into an area now known as Smith's Cove, about five hundred feet east of the Money Pit. Upon further exploration, the workers discovered that the beach bordering Smith's Cove was completely artificial. When they shoveled out the sand and gravel, they discovered a layer of coconut fiber, another one of eelgrass, and a third of beach rocks. It became clear that this cleverly designed beach was a mechanism for keeping the Money Pit flooded. A later team of workers found that two flood tunnels — one from Smith's Cove and another from South Shore Cove — had been built to intersect with the Money Pit, ensuring that if it was tampered with, the shaft would flood with seawater, making further exploration impossible.

In the years since the deaths of Vaughan and Smith, almost every technique has been used to reach the bottom of the Money Pit. Skin divers were employed, and

WHAT'S IN THE MONEY PIT?

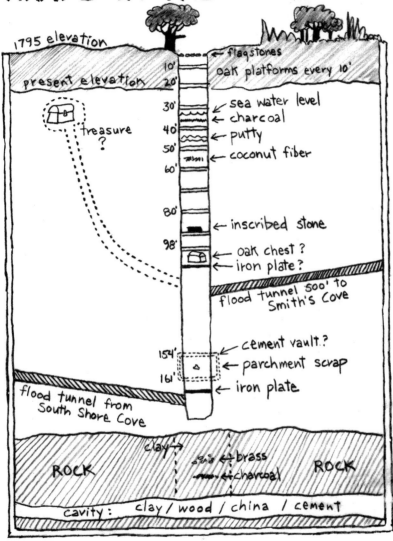

1795 elevation

present elevation

10'
20'
30'
40'
50'
60'
80'
98'

154'
161'

treasure
?

flagstones
oak platforms every 10'

← sea water level
← charcoal
← putty
← coconut fiber

← inscribed stone

← oak chest ?
← iron plate ?

flood tunnel 500' to
Smith's Cove

← cement vault ?
← parchment scrap
← iron plate

flood tunnel from
South Shore Cove

ROCK

clay →

brass
charcoal

ROCK

cavity : clay / wood / china / cement

even giant pumps were imported. But the cost of draining the pit was too high for one person. The hunt has therefore been turned over to companies who sell stock shares to raise money for men and equipment. When the money runs out, as it always does, the excavations stop for years at a time until another group raises funds for another attempt. So many explorations of Oak Island have taken place that the location of the original Money Pit is no longer known. The island is pockmarked with shafts and tunnels. What was once a beautiful wooded area now looks more like a toxic waste dump.

But the biggest problem with the Money Pit is the name the three young men initially gave it. From the very beginning, they assumed that a large cache of treasure was buried. Almost every person involved in the two hundred years of excavation has made the same assumption, based on very little evidence. Other than scraps of wood and coconut fiber or — once — a small bit of parchment, no tangible evidence exists to show that something was buried there. Yet wood taken from shaft has been scientifically dated to around 1575 A.D., plus or minus eighty-five years. If the wood was part of a construction, it was built almost one hundred years before Daniel McGinnis stepped onto Oak Island. Someone may have dug a pit and filled it in, someone may have built a structure — but this doesn't mean that a treasure was buried in it.

What about the strange stone with the mysterious inscription? Doesn't it prove that a treasure exists? The

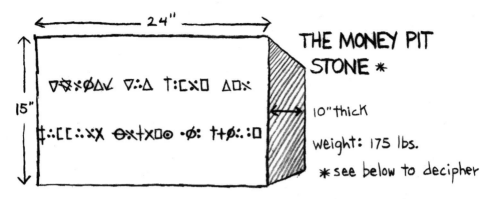

THE MONEY PIT STONE *

10" thick

weight: 175 lbs.

* see below to decipher

stone, however, was either misplaced or stolen around 1919. In 1865, the inscription supposedly was decoded by a professor at Dalhousie University. It read, in an easily deciphered code, *Forty feet below two million pounds are buried.* Many people are skeptical of this translation, especially since it was used to raise more money for the excavation. Because the stone no longer exists, there is also no proof that the inscription was real.

Despite this lack of evidence, many associated with the Money Pit have sacrificed their fortunes and their lives for their single-minded pursuit of the possible treasure. Some researchers are not convinced that a pirate treasure will be found under Oak Island. Rather, they believe that the Spanish or English government buried a huge amount of stolen Inca treasure there. Others theorize that Francis Bacon buried information there that would prove he really wrote the plays attributed to William Shakespeare. And a few others support the idea that a large UFO base was once located beneath Oak Island.

CODE to the STONE

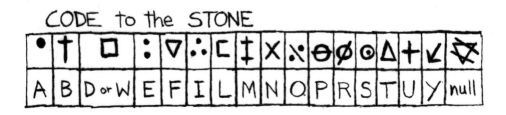

As you can see, without proof one idea is as good as another. And yet the searches for a large treasure continue. They are now conducted by Triton Alliance, which sells stock in the hope of raising $10,000,000 to fund the next excavation. Daniel McGinnis and his friends probably never imagined this result.

Another legendary treasure that has led many astray and ruined many lives is the Lost Dutchman Mine, supposedly located in the Superstition Mountains east of Phoenix, Arizona. As with most legends, there are many discrepancies among the various accounts. According to Helen Corbin, author of *The Curse of the Dutchman's Gold*, in 1846, a man named Jacob Waltz emigrated from Wurttemberg, Germany, to the United States. After he became a naturalized American citizen in July 1861, he traveled to Arizona and became a prospector. Sometime between 1872 and 1878, Waltz and his partner, Jacob Weisner, reportedly found gold in an eighteen-inch-wide vein of quartz. They mined some ore and placed

172

it in a cache near the mine. One day, while working on the mine, Weisner was killed by the Apaches. Upset by Weisner's death, Waltz never filed a claim for the mine. He concealed its entrance, took only the ore that he needed to live on, and moved to Phoenix, where he lived in an adobe house on a small farm near the Salt River.

There, he earned his living by delivering fresh eggs to a woman named Julia Thomas, who owned a local bakery and knew nothing of Waltz's mine. One day in 1891, Waltz discovered that Julia was in debt and in danger of losing her bakery, and he offered to help her repay her debts. Until the moment that he showed her gold ore worth about $1,500, Julia thought he was a poor farmer.

Waltz told her that he would ship the gold to a smelter in San Francisco. "I've shipped gold from Casa Grande in the past," he said. "I'm familiar with the procedure. When the money comes back, I'll lend most of it to you."

He continued:

There's a great deal more where that came from. . . . It's in a cache that we made, my partner and I. The gold came out of a mine, of course. I have the right to work that mine, but I gave that up after my partner was killed. He was killed by the Apaches twenty years ago, and I never wanted to work in the mine again. Anyway, I'm getting too old for that kind of thing now.

He promised to share the wealth of the mine with Julia and her adopted son, Rhinehart Petrasch. They planned a trip into the Superstitions during the spring of 1892 to retrieve the rest of the gold in Waltz's cache. Unfortunately, Waltz's house was swamped that summer when the normally dry Salt River was flooded with run-off from torrential rains. Waltz caught pneumonia from his drenching and died on October 25, 1891, months before he could take Julia and Rhinehart into the Super-stitions. Shortly before his death, he reportedly told them that a small amount of gold ore was hidden be-neath his fireplace and he sketched a map giving the

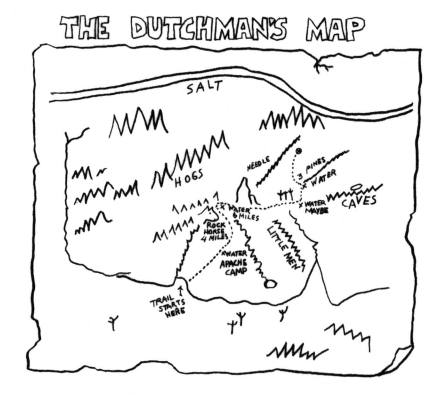

location of the mine. Not only did they not find the mine, they were even robbed of the gold ore that Waltz had left them.

The bare-bones account of this story has been enough to send thousands of treasure hunters into the Superstitions, where some have died, sometimes under mysterious and rather gruesome circumstances. Just as it did among the Oak Island searchers, greed replaced common sense — except in a few treasure trackers.

One searcher who took a different approach is Bob Corbin, who has hunted for the legendary mine since 1957. As a child in rural Indiana, Corbin wasn't particularly interested in finding treasure, but while serving in the Navy around 1948, he read a magazine article about the fabled mine. The article interested Corbin enough to change the course of his life: he decided to move to Arizona and tackle the Lost Dutchman.

A greedy treasure hunter would have made plans to head for Arizona immediately, but not Corbin. He had obviously learned something from the mistakes of many others. Searching for the Lost Dutchman Mine was to become his hobby, not his primary occupation. First, after leaving the Navy, he went home and earned a college degree at Indiana University. After that, he completed a law degree.

Only then, in June 1957, nine years after he had decided to look for the Lost Dutchman Mine, did Corbin move to Arizona, ready to practice law and start his treasure-hunting hobby. On his first weekend there, he went into the Superstition Mountains. As an inexperienced desert dweller, he hadn't thought much about Arizona summers. He quickly learned that the best time to prospect was winter, when temperatures were lower and ground water was plentiful. He also learned that further research was in order.

But he had work to do. Besides occasional trips into the Superstitions, Corbin was a county attorney and eventually served as the Arizona attorney general from 1979 to 1991. Even with such demanding jobs, Corbin found time to pursue his hobby.

He and his partner, Tom Kollenborn, have spent more than thirty years poring over documents and old newspapers, trying to prove the basic outline of Jacob Waltz's story. During this time, Corbin went through different phases. Sometimes he believed the mine was real, sometimes not. Once, when he doubted its existence, he did not set foot in the Superstitions for seven years. Now, however, the two partners' research has convinced him that there is a mine, although it has been filled in or otherwise obscured.

Many treasure trackers would be disappointed at not finding a gold mine after thirty years' work, but not Corbin. What he enjoys is the search. It gives him the opportunity to get outdoors, away from the pressures of work, and the chance to sit by a campfire, cooking his dinner and gazing at a wide sky. After all, Corbin ex-

plained, "you can see so many more stars in the mountains."

What's more, he has developed a hobby that builds on his skills as a lawyer. In both instances, he sifts through evidence, looking for facts, checking for discrepancies. He follows up on hunches and asks tough questions. In his vocation *and* his avocation, he relies on his inquisitive mind, as all successful treasure trackers should.

If you want to be successful, you will want to avoid hunting for treasures like the one that may — or may not — be found on Oak Island. The cost will probably never equal the reward.

You may prefer to be more like Bob Corbin and look for a large treasure, not really caring whether you find it. You may want to wait until you're an adult with a full-time job. Then you can spend your spare time and your spare change on your hobby, trying to prove that the treasure exists, appreciating the pleasures that a curious mind can bring.

Or perhaps you prefer to begin your search now. . . .

If you do, start searching for a small treasure. As you look, enjoy your trip on the treasure trail. When you discover something, consider how it came to be there. Wonder about the person who owned it. Imagine his or her face and clothes, feelings and dreams. And know that one day, someone may be holding an object you once owned . . . and thinking of you.

Appendix

**Sample Search Agreement Between Treasure Tracker
and Landowner**

Date _____
      Month   Day   Year

Name of Treasure Tracker: _____

Name of Landowner: _____

Property to be searched: _____

Method of search: _____

Treasure sought: _____

   The Landowner hereby agrees to allow the Treasure Tracker to search the property for a period of _____(hours, days, weeks [circle one])

If the Treasure Tracker finds any money, jewelry, artifacts, or other treasure, the Landowner will receive _____ percent of the finds as payment. The Treasure Tracker agrees not to damage the property in any way.

Other terms to be specified:_____
_____
_____

Signed _____ _____
      Treasure Tracker   Landowner

For Further Reading

General Treasure Stories

Charley, Catherine. *Hunting for Treasure*. London: Salamander, 1990.

Donnelly, Judy. *True-Life Treasure Hunts*. New York: Random House, 1984.

Haydock, Tim. *Treasure Trove: Where to Find the Great Lost Treasures of the World*. New York: Holt, 1986.

Madison, Arnold. *Lost Treasures of America*. Chicago: Rand McNally, 1977.

Nesmith, Robert L. *Dig for Pirate Treasure*. New York: Bonanza Books, 1958.

Norman, Bruce. *Footsteps: Nine Archaeological Journeys of Romance and Discovery*. London: BBC Books, 1987.

Norvill, Roy. *The Treasure Seeker's Treasury*. London: Hutchinson, 1978.

Snow, Edward Rowe. *True Tales of Pirates and Their Gold*. New York: Dutton, 1953.

Titler, Dale M. *Unnatural Resources: True Stories of American Treasure*. Englewood Cliffs: Prentice-Hall, 1973.

Tompkins, B. A., ed. *Treasure: Man's 25 Greatest Quests for Eldorado*. New York: Times Books, 1979.

Trease, Geoffrey. *Hidden Treasure*. London: Hamish Hamilton, 1989.

Williams, Adam. *Missing Treasure*. Windermere: Ray Rourke Publishing, 1981.

Wilson, Ian. *Undiscovered*. New York: William Morrow, 1987.

182

Treasure-Hunting Tips

Garrett, Charles, and Roy Lagal. *Modern Treasure Hunting.* Dallas: Ram Publishing, 1988.

Madison, Arnold. *Treasure Hunting.* New York: Hawthorn Books, 1974.

McIntosh, Jane. *The Archaeologist's Handbook.* London: Bell and Hyman, 1986.

Codes and Ciphers

Mango, Karen N. *Codes, Ciphers, and Other Secrets.* New York: Franklin Watts, 1988.

Acknowledgments

spanish doubloon

My own treasure hunt for this book required visits to many libraries in the United States and England. I wish to thank librarians at the New York Public Library, the Library of Congress, the Phoenix and Scottsdale (Arizona) Public Libraries, the Arizona State University Library, and the University of New Mexico Library for their assistance. I am also indebted to Gary Ferguson of the State of Louisiana Library who helped me track down one rare book, and Marian Fry of the Arbury Park Branch Library in Cambridge, England, who was generous with the use of her library card when I discovered another. Special thanks are also in order to Michael Paul Henson, who answered my many inquiries.

In writing this book, I have used the books and articles listed below. Although most were written for adults, some are suitable for younger readers. These are marked with an asterisk (*).

Allen, Floyd. "Gold Fever." *Treasure*, September 1991: 6–8.

Ater, Bob. "Doodle Bugging: Methods for the Modern Dowser." *Treasure*, October 1989: 28–29, 77.

Barrett, John G. *The Civil War in North Carolina*. Chapel Hill: University of North Carolina Press, 1963.

Black, Clinton V. *Pirates of the West Indies*. Cambridge: Cambridge University Press, 1989.

184

Brewer, James D. "The Mystery of the Civil War Locket." *Lost Treasure*, August 1985: 14–15.

Brooks, Ken. "Custer's Navy: The Tragic Journey of the Sternwheeler *Far West*." *True West*, October 1986: 14–21.

Bruner, James. "Treasure Sites Often Overlooked." *Lost Treasure*, May 1990: 36–39.

Burgess, Robert F. *Sinkings, Salvages, and Shipwrecks*. New York: American Heritage Press, 1970.

Carl and Bill. "Sabinal's Silver Found!" *Treasure*, November 1990: 27–28, 48–49, 65.

Carlisle, Norman, and David Michelsohn. *The Complete Guide to Treasure Hunting*. Chicago: Henry Regnery, 1973.

Carson, H. Glenn. "Practical Treasure Hunting Tips." *Western & Eastern Treasures*, November 1990: 74–75.

Casteneda, Tony. "Capt. Nemo, the Gold Horse, & Me." *Treasure*, March 1990: 48–56.

Chaplan, Michael. "New York City Cache Hunt." *Western & Eastern Treasures*, February 1991: 59–61.

Charroux, Robert. *Treasures of the World*. Trans. Gloria Cantu. New York: Eriksson, 1966.

Clark, Joe. "Slingshot Ammo." *Western & Eastern Treasures*, November 1990: 72–73.

Corbin, Helen. *The Curse of the Dutchman's Gold*. Phoenix: Foxwest Publishing, 1990.

Corbin, Robert K. Interview. 22 April 1991.

Curran, Harold. *Fearful Crossing: The Central Overland Trail through Nevada*. Las Vegas: Nevada Publications, 1982.

Daniloff, Ruth. "A Cipher's the Key to the Treasure in Them Thar Hills." *Smithsonian*, April 1981: 126–44.

Duffy, Howard M. "$50,000 at the Crossroads." *Treasure*, March 1990: 7–8.

———. "The Value of Research." *Treasure*, January 1990: 30–31.

Eberhart, Perry. *Treasure Tales of the Rockies*. Denver: Sage Books, 1961.

Farmer, Hardrock Rick. "Caching in a Silver Hoard." *Treasure*, December 1989: 54–56.

Freeman, Patricia, with Dirk Mathison. "Writer D'Arcy O'Connor, Digging Deep into 'Money Pit' Lore, Unearths a Trove of Mysteries." *People*, March 6, 1989: 235–36.

Furneaux, Rupert. *Great Treasure Hunts*. Feltham, England: Old-hams, 1969.

Harris, Charles S. "Bobby Barnes: The Second Time Around." *Treasure*, August 1990: 26–29.

Hawkins, Bruce R., and David B. Madsen. *Excavation of the Donner-Reed Wagons: Historic Archaeology along the Hastings Cut-off*. Salt Lake City: University of Utah Press, 1990.

Henson, Michael Paul. "Quest for Silver Ends in Tragedy." *Lost Treasure*, April 1984: 24–25.

Hiott, David. "Ponds Produce Good Coinshooting Site." *Western & Eastern Treasures*, November 1990: 24, 26.

Hoffman, Paul. *Archimedes' Revenge: The Joys and Perils of Mathematics*. New York: Norton, 1988.

———. "Explorations." *Omni*, May 1987: 24.

Irons, Angie. "Little Treasures from Post-Hole Banks." *Lost Treasure*, May 1990: 14–15.

Irwin, John D., Jr. "Treasures from the Plow." *Treasure*, February 1990: 24–26, 34.

Jolley, Brad. "Dr. Crypton's Golden Horse Laugh." *Treasure*, April 1990: 42–49.

Longo, William R. "Weird Water Discoveries." *Treasure*, July 1990, 52–57.

Martin, Richard. "Out of the Way Metal Detecting Spots." *Lost Treasure*, May 1990: 19–22.

McGlashan, C. F. *History of the Donner Party, 1881*. Stanford: Stanford University Press, 1947.

Molnar, Tom. "Detectors on Donner Summit." *Treasure*, January 1991: 38–40.

———. "Wagon Trail Treasure: The Fruits of Searching the Middle of Nowhere." *Treasure*, August 1990: 44–45, 75.

*O'Connor, D'Arcy. *The Big Dig*. New York: Ballantine, 1988.

Palmore, Frank E. "Gold at Rock Crossing." *Treasure*, October 1989, 49–51.

Preston, Douglas. "Death Trap Defies Treasure Seekers for Two Centuries." *Smithsonian*, June 1988: 52–64.

Reid, Alistair. "Digging up Scotland." *The New Yorker*, October 5, 1981: 59–125.

Renan, Sheldon. "The Making of the Golden Horse." *Treasure*, January 1990: 50–62.

———. *Treasure*. New York: Warner, 1984.

Ritchie, Robert C. *Captain Kidd and the War against the Pirates*. Cambridge, Mass.: Harvard University Press, 1986.

Roden, Hans. *Treasure-Seekers*. Trans. Frances Hogarth-Gaute. New York: Walker, 1963.

Sandness, John. "Clean up at the Carwash." *Lost Treasure*, May 1990: 16–17.

*Saxon, Lyle. *Lafitte the Pirate*. New York: Century, 1930.

Schurmacher, Emile C. *Lost Treasures and How to Find Them!* New York: Paperback Library, 1968.

Shafer, Louis S. "Mystery of the 3 Gravestones." *Treasure*, November 1989: 43–47.

Smith, John D. "Proper Research: The Key to Success." *Treasure*, October 1990: 40–41.

Sterling, Mick, and Arlene Amodei. "Locating the Donner Families' Camps." *Western & Eastern Treasures*, December 1990: 37–38.

Stewart, George R. *The California Trail, 1962*. Lincoln: University of Nebraska Press, 1983.

———. *Ordeal by Hunger: The Story of the Donner Party, 1936*. Lincoln: University of Nebraska Press, 1986.

Stockbridge, Jack. Interview. Tapes no. 388 and 402. With Lou Blachly. Pioneer Foundation, Inc. Special Collections Department, University of New Mexico General Library, Albuquerque.

Thrower, Rayner. *The Pirate Picture*. London: Phillimore, 1980.

Tosaw, Richard T. "D. B. Cooper — Dead or Alive?" *Lost Treasure*, July 1985: 18–21.

Tower, Howard B. "Research + Interviews = Treasure." *Lost Treasure*, January 1985: 46–47.

Vance, Tom. "Arrowheads Go Undetected." *Lost Treasure*, January 1982: 60–65.

Verrill, A. Hyatt. *They Found Gold*. Glorieta: Rio Grande Press, 1972.

*Viemeister, Peter. *The Beale Treasure: A History of a Mystery*. Bedford: Hamilton's, 1987.

Viles, Donald. "Looting the Jacksonville Bank." *Lost Treasure*, March 1991: 19–21.

Von Mueller, Karl. *Treasure Hunter's Manual #7*. Dallas: Ram Publishing, 1979.

Wagner, Kip, as told to L. B. Taylor, Jr. *Pieces of Eight*. New York: Dutton, 1966.

Weir, T. C. "Found: One Ring." *Treasure*, August 1990: 6–7.

Wetherill, Benjamin Alfred. *The Wetherills of the Mesa Verde*. Lincoln: University of Nebraska Press, 1987.

Yeager, C. G. *Arrowheads and Stone Artifacts*. Boulder, Col.: Pruett Publishing, 1986.

Index

Albert, Alphaeus H.   60–61
Alder Creek   63–67
Allen, Floyd   74
Allen, Joe   111
Applegate Trail   109
Artifacts   59
Atocha   36

Barnes, Bobby   109
Beachcombing   75
Beale ciphers   17–25
Beale Cypher Association   26
Beale Papers, The   20
Beale, Thomas   13–18, 20–22
Beekman Bank   103
Benuit, Joni   32
Bighorn River   158, 161
Blachly, Lou   97
Blue Ridge Mountains   16
Brewer, James   47–49
Bruff, J. Goldsborough   107
Bruner, James   155
Burial treasure   68
Buried Treasure of the United States   98
Burns, Jimmy   97
Burying treasure   150
Buzzard's treasure   84

Cache   50
Carter Cave State Resort Park   39
Chaplan, Michael   126–127
Cherokee   39–40, 77
Ciphers   140
   substitution   141
   key-word   143

Cliff Palace   129
Clues to treasure site   101
   ghost towns   102
   local legends   116
   public places   110
   robbers' caches   112
   transportation routes   105
Columbus (Ohio) *Dispatch*   89
Columbia River   114–115
Cooper, Dan   112–115
Corbin, Bob   175–177
Corbin, Helen   172
Criminal treasure   54
Cruise-Wilkins, Reginald   38
Curse of the Dutchman's Gold   172
Custer, General George
      Armstrong   157–158

Dalhousie University   171
Declaration of Independence   18
Deppenschmit, Kurt   59
Donner Lake   63
Donner Memorial State Park   64, 66
Donner Party   62
Dowsing   82
   remote   82
   site   83
Dr. Crypton   86
Dreaming   89
Duffy, Howard M.   38–39, 116

Eberhart, Perry   56
Elizabeth Ann Seton School   86
Elkins, George   56
Erie Canal   109

189

Far West (steamboat) 158
Farmer, Hardrock Rick 41
Fisher, Mel 36
Fletcher, Alonso 89

Ghost towns 102–104
Gilmore, Leon 77
Golden Horse Treasure Hunt 86
Golden rules of treasure
    tracking 44–46
Gray, Clint 83–84
Gulf Coast 32

Haggman, Henry 50–53
Hardesty, Don 65–67
Hatton, Tom 56
Hauptmann, Bruno Richard 126
Hawkins, Bruce 64
Henson, Michael Paul 39
Hidden treasure 50
Hiott, David 111
Historical artifacts 58
Historical information 62
Hodder, Cecil 133
Hoffman, Paul 86
Houston (Texas) Treasure and Relic
    Hunters Club 110
Huraken 39

Ingram family 114
Interstate 495 53
Irons, Angie 79
Irwin, John D., Jr. 59–61

Jefferson, Arthur 102–104
Jolley, Brad 87

Kerchner, Helen 87
Kid Johnson 118
Kidd, Captain William 31, 163, 164,
    165

King Louis XV 37
Kollenborn, Tom 176

Lafitte, Jean 26, 32
Lang, Stan 80
Laws concerning treasure 49, 53, 57
Le Vasseur, Oliver 37
Lerner, Jeff 151–152
Lewis brothers 102–104
library tips 93–99
Lindbergh kidnapping 126
Lindemann, William 66
Little Bighorn 158, 161
Local history collection 96
Local legends 116
Location of treasures
    Averasboro, North Carolina 47
    Belen, New Mexico 118
    Bighorn River, Montana 158, 161
    Bolton, Massachusetts 52–53
    Carter County, Kentucky 39
    Chesapeake Bay, Maryland 76
    Cheyenne, Wyoming 80
    Clifford, Colorado 55–57
    Cold Spring, New Jersey 31
    Columbia River,
        Washington 114–115
    Danville, Vermont 83
    Gallipolis, Ohio 89
    Glen Innes, Australia 105
    Great Salt Lake Desert, Utah 62
    Greenville, South Carolina 111
    Houston, Texas 110
    Hunter Island, New York 126
    Isle au Haut, Maine 50, 52
    Jackson, Tennessee 116
    Jacksonville, Oregon 102
    Lynchburg, Virginia 13
    Mahé, Seychelles Islands 37–38
    Mancheng, China 68
    Mancos, Colorado 129

Matagorda Island, Texas   32, 33
Nottoway Courthouse, Virginia   48
Oak Island, Nova Scotia   163
Rabbit Hole Springs,
   Nevada   106–107
Rock Crossing, Texas   124–125
Salt Lake City, Utah   41
Santa Fe, New Mexico   16
Silver City, New Mexico   97
Snettisham, England   133
St. Andrews, Scotland   151
Superstition Mountains   172
Trenton, New Jersey   60
Tulsa, Oklahoma   77
Wabasso, Florida   35
Waikiki, Hawaii   131
Longo, William   76
Lost treasure   47
Lost Treasure (magazine)   95

Madsen, David   64
Manuita   39
Marsh, Captain Grant   158–161
Martin, Laddie   41
Martin, Richard   105, 155
Marx, Robert F.   98, 110
Masquerade   85
McCormick, Thomas   89
McGinnis, Daniel   163–172
McGlashan, C. F.   64
Mesa Verde National Park   130
Metal detecting   73
Miller, J. P.   81
Molnar, Tom   106–108
Money Pit   165–171
Morriss, Robert   13–17, 20–22

Natchez Trace Trail   109
National Forest Service   61
National Park Service   61
Newspaper microfilms   95

Norvill, Roy   159–161
Nuestra Señora de Atocha   36

O'Kane, Richard   132–133
Oral history collection   96
Orchard, David   105
Oregon Trail   109

Palmore, Frank   125
Palmore, Lewis Franklin   124–125
Patterson, Doug   47–49
Petrasch, Rhinehart   174
Pioneer Palace   64
Pioneers Foundation   96
Pope, Floyd   48
Prince Liu Sheng   68–69
Princess Dou Wan   68–69
Puzzle solving   84

*Record of American Uniform and Historical
   Buttons*   60
Reed, Virginia   64
Reid family   150–152
Renan, Sheldon   86
Ritchie, Robert C.   30
Robbers' caches   112
Roosevelt, Teddy   97
Rules of treasure hunting   121–123

Savy, Mrs. Charles   37
Schaffner, Florence   112
Schurmacher, Emile   159
Schutts, Wayne   131–132
Sioux   160
Sisco, Phillip   77
Skyjacking   112
Smith, Janie   47
Smith, John   165–168
Smith, Reg   83
Snow, Edward Rowe   32–34
Stevenson, Robert Louis   21

Stewart, George R.   107
Stockbridge, Jack   96–98
Stout, Dick   101

Techniques for tracking treasure   72
  beachcombing   75
  dowsing   82
  dreaming   89
  metal detecting   73
  puzzle solving   84
  visual searching   77
Thomas, Julia   173–174
Thompson, Dick   31
Tosaw, Richard   115
Transportation routes   105
Treasure (book)   86
Treasure (magazine)   87, 95
Treasure Island   31
Treasure maps   137–140
Treasure report   128
Treasure traps   28
Treasure types   44
  burial treasure   68
  criminal treasure   54
  hidden treasure   50
  historical artifacts   59
  historical information   62
  lost treasure   47

Vance, Tom   77
Vaughan, Anthony   165–168
Viles, Donald   102
Visual searching   77
  arrowheads   77
  fence posts   78
  drainage systems   80
  garage sales   81

Wagner, Kip   35
Waltz, Jacob   172–175
Ward, James   20
Washington, George   61
Weisner, Jacob   172–173
Western & Eastern Treasures (magazine)   95
Wetherill, Benjamin Alfred   129–130
Will, James   56
Williams, Kit   85–86
Woolfork family   116–117
Wooten, Joe   32

XYZ   17–22

Yeager, C. G.   78

spanish
piece of eight